BLESSING OF THE GODS

Picking up the bunch of spring flowers that Lord Springdale had bought on his way to Chelsea, Ben hurried into the hospital.

Holding the reins in his hands, Lord Springdale was now making himself comfortable in the driving seat when suddenly he was aware that someone had climbed into the chaise beside him and a woman's voice now said,

"Drive away – as quickly as you can!"

It was an order.

As he turned to look at the speaker, he saw that she was a young and very attractive girl.

As he gazed at her, she turned her head to look back at the entrance to the hospital with dread.

"Hurry! Hurry!" she cried. "We must get away as fast as we can."

Because the young girl was being so insistent, Lord Springdale, instead of arguing, did as she requested.

The horses were only too eager to oblige by moving as rapidly as possible down the road in front of him.

THE BARBARA CARTLAND PINK COLLECTION

Titles in this series

BLESSING OF THE GODS

BARBARA CARTLAND

Barbaracartland.com Ltd

THE BARBARA CARTLAND PINK COLLECTION

Dame Barbara Cartland is still regarded as the most prolific bestselling author in the history of the world.

In her lifetime she was frequently in the Guinness Book of Records for writing more books than any other living author.

Her most amazing literary feat was to double her output from 10 books a year to over 20 books a year when she was 77 to meet the huge demand.

She went on writing continuously at this rate for 20 years and wrote her very last book at the age of 97, thus completing an incredible 400 books between the ages of 77 and 97.

Her publishers finally could not keep up with this phenomenal output, so at her death in 2000 she left behind an amazing 160 unpublished manuscripts, something that no other author has ever achieved.

Barbara's son, Ian McCorquodale, together with his daughter Iona, felt that it was their sacred duty to publish all these titles for Barbara's millions of admirers all over the world who so love her wonderful romances.

So in 2004 they started publishing the 160 brand new Barbara Cartlands as *The Barbara Cartland Pink Collection*, as Barbara's favourite colour was always pink – and yet more pink!

The Barbara Cartland Pink Collection is published monthly exclusively by Barbaracartland.com and the books are numbered in sequence from 1 to 160.

Enjoy receiving a brand new Barbara Cartland book each month by taking out an annual subscription to the Pink Collection, or purchase the books individually.

The Pink Collection is available from the Barbara Cartland website www.barbaracartland.com via mail order and through all good bookshops.

In addition Ian and Iona are proud to announce that The Barbara Cartland Pink Collection is now available in ebook format as from Valentine's Day 2011.

For more information, please contact us at:

Barbaracartland.com Ltd.
Camfield Place
Hatfield
Hertfordshire AL9 6JE
United Kingdom

Telephone: +44 (0)1707 642629
Fax: +44 (0)1707 663041
Email: info@barbaracartland.com

THE LATE DAME BARBARA CARTLAND

Barbara Cartland who sadly died in May 2000 at the age of nearly 99 was the world's most famous romantic novelist who wrote 723 books in her lifetime with worldwide sales of over 1 billion copies and her books were translated into 36 different languages.

As well as romantic novels, she wrote historical biographies, 6 autobiographies, theatrical plays, books of advice on life, love, vitamins and cookery. She also found time to be a political speaker and television and radio personality.

She wrote her first book at the age of 21 and this was called *Jigsaw*. It became an immediate bestseller and sold 100,000 copies in hardback and was translated into 6 different languages. She wrote continuously throughout her life, writing bestsellers for an astonishing 76 years. Her books have always been immensely popular in the United States, where in 1976 her current books were at numbers 1 & 2 in the B. Dalton bestsellers list, a feat never achieved before or since by any author.

Barbara Cartland became a legend in her own lifetime and will be best remembered for her wonderful romantic novels, so loved by her millions of readers throughout the world.

Her books will always be treasured for their moral message, her pure and innocent heroines, her good looking and dashing heroes and above all her belief that the power of love is more important than anything else in everyone's life.

"When I was married, I felt that God was blessing me and my husband and our love. The angels were singing and the gates of Paradise were opening for me. It will be the same for you."

Barbara Cartland

CHAPTER ONE
1882

"It's Lord Springdale, my Lady," the nurse called out when she answered a knock on the door.

The woman in bed gave a cry of joy.

"Oh, please let him come in."

The nurse opened the door and Lord Springdale, who was a tall very good-looking young man, walked in.

He came across the room and his grandmother held out both her arms as she said,

"Oh, Ian, I am so glad to see you and it is so kind of you to come."

"Of course I came at once," he replied. "I only got back from Scotland yesterday and so I had no idea that you were in a hospital until the butler told me."

"I did not want you to be worried while you were enjoying yourself with your friends," his grandmother said. "But now you have come I feel better already. It was only because the doctors fuss so much that I let them bring me in here at all."

"I think it is very wise," Lord Springdale remarked, "and I have heard that this is a very comfortable hospital."

He had also heard, although he did not say so, that it was a very snobbish one.

They definitely liked to have important people and aristocrats as their patients.

Equally he would always want his grandmother, to whom he was devoted, to have the best.

"Now tell me about your visit to me," she asked.

As she was sitting up in bed, he thought she looked, not ill, but actually better than when she had been rushing about as she always liked to do, entertaining and helping her endless list of charitable causes.

"First I need to know about you, Grandmama," he said. "It was a terrible shock when I arrived home and learnt that you had been taken away and was here in this hospital."

"It is really only the doctors fussing over me," his grandmother replied. "I could perfectly well have had a nurse at home. But they thought it would be better if I was here. What they actually meant was that it was better and easier for them!"

Her grandson laughed.

"I can believe that," he answered. "Now promise me that you are really getting well and will soon be coming back to the house as it is not the same without you."

His grandmother looked satisfied.

He knew that she loved being with him in the large house in Berkeley Square that had been in the family for several generations.

Not as long as the house in the country where his Lordship had been born and which now belonged to him although he always spoke as if she was still in charge of it.

"Now tell me about your party with your friends," Lady Springdale suggested. "I am bored with talking about myself."

"Then you are the only woman who can say that," her grandson laughed. "The women where I was staying were, in fact, a perfect nuisance because they only wanted to talk about themselves and were not interested as I was in the horses and the sport."

There was silence for a moment.

Then Lady Springdale volunteered,

"I rather hoped that you would be bringing me good news."

Her grandson groaned.

"If you really thought that I would propose to that exceedingly dull daughter of my host, you are very much mistaken. I was very fond of her brother, as you do know, because we were at Eton and Oxford together but, although I did not say so to him, his sister is a crashing bore!"

His grandmother sighed.

"Oh, Ian, I thought she was rather nice and because you were keen on staying with the family I foolishly hoped that you had other reasons for going there."

"Then you were very wrong," Lord Springdale said. "What is more, Grandmama, I can tell you here and now, I have no intention of marrying anyone!"

His grandmother gave a cry of horror.

"My dear boy, you are nearly twenty-seven and you must have an heir. You know as well as I do if anything happened to you there would be no one to carry on as Head of the Family and your title would die out completely."

"I wonder if that would matter so much fifty years from now?" he questioned with a touch of sarcasm in his voice.

"Of course it would matter," she replied. "We have always been so proud of being an old family. Moreover we have played a huge part in the history of England, at least we can be proud of our name and we have done our best in a quiet way to help our beloved country to become an example to all the others in Europe."

Her grandson had heard this all before.

In fact it was one of her favourite speeches.

He therefore said nothing.

And then after a rather uncomfortable silence Lady Springdale said,

"Now listen to me, dearest Ian, you must realise how important your position is. So, if you do not produce a son, then the title will be discontinued and our name will die out. All we have achieved in the past centuries will be forgotten and lost in the sands of time."

He did not think that his family had done all that much, but he was too polite to say so.

Instead he said quietly,

"I am sorry to disappoint you, Grandmama, but I really have no wish to be married at the moment."

"But you do see, my dearest boy, that, as you are getting older and I am afraid more particular, you may not have the heir who is so vital to our family's future."

Her grandson did not speak.

And after a moment Lady Springdale sighed deeply and then went on,

"As you will well know it has always been a bitter disappointment to me and to your grandfather when he was alive that we only had one son, your father. As you know after you were born, your mother was unable to have any more children."

She sighed again before she added,

"I longed to have a good number of grandchildren, but alas my daughter, as you know, married an Italian and lives in Italy. She only managed to produce three girls. It broke my heart that she did not come back here to England. And you will know over the years that I have seen very little of my granddaughters."

He had heard all this a thousand times before.

But, because he was so fond of his grandmother, he took her hand in his and said soothingly,

"You have been such a wonderful grandmother and no one could ever blame you for not having the number of grandchildren you want. But I promise you I will always be a devoted grandson and you must not force me into a life that I know I would dislike intensely until I do find the right woman to share it with."

"But, dearest, you said all this last year and the year before," his grandmother persisted. "I did so hope that you would bring me good news by now."

"I am sorry, Grandmama, but I absolutely refuse to marry someone I don't like and who has no attraction for me simply because you crave grandchildren."

Despite herself Lady Springdale laughed.

"That does sound a little odd," she replied. "At the same time it happens to be the truth."

"Well, it's a game I am not playing at the moment." But when I do find this wonderful woman, who will look delightful in your tiara when you lend it to her, I promise you, you will be the first one to congratulate me."

"That is very poor comfort," she answered. "It's a promise you have made to me so often before."

"Yes, I know, Grandmama. In fact ever since I was twenty-one you have tried resolutely to force me up the aisle with some tiresome young woman, who I know only too well would bore me stiff the moment the honeymoon was over."

"How can you say that, dearest?" his grandmother questioned. "After all there are masses of very pretty girls in London, who I am certain would be only too pleased if you were attracted by them."

She was reflecting as she spoke that, although her grandson was unaware of it, she knew that he had been having a number of *affaires-de-coeur* with married women who were undoubtedly the Queens of the Social world and who entertained all the attractive gentlemen in London.

They were far more amusing and fun than whole bevies of innocent young *debutantes*.

Lady Springdale had, in fact, two or three friends who told her exactly who her grandson was interested in at present.

Invariably after a very short passionate love affair, he would drift away to find someone new, while, according to them, the woman he had left behind wept bitterly.

His grandmother naturally has been far too tactful to mention this to him.

But, when he had finished his last *affaire-de-coeur*, she was delighted at the news and so hoped that this was the moment when he would finally settle down and marry someone who would produce an heir.

"So what are you going to do now that you are back in London, Ian?" Lady Springdale asked him aloud.

She was hoping that he would tell her the truth, but thought it unlikely.

"I don't know," he answered. "When I came back, I found a huge pile of invitations, but I have not had time to peruse them. They seem to me much of a muchness."

"What you really mean," his grandmother said, "is that they are being given for the girls who are coming out this Season and you are really looking as you have before, for someone older and – perhaps more experienced."

This was something that he had not heard from his grandmother in the past.

He laughed before he chided her,

"Now, Grandmama, you are being very curious. I can assure you that there is no one at the moment who I find more attractive than you and that is why I have come straight here, having only arrived home just before dinner last night."

"I am very touched you should do so, my dear boy. At the same time I had hoped, as you were away so long, that you would have the news I am so anxious to hear."

"You said that already," he replied. "Quite frankly there was no one there you would have thought, if you had seen them, attractive to me."

His grandmother sighed.

"I just cannot imagine what you are looking for, an angel from Heaven perhaps? Or must she be someone so sensational and so completely different in every way that you are bowled over by her."

"Now you are putting words into my mouth that I have not actually said, Grandmama. Actually, if I did get married, it would be someone exceptional like yourself and honestly they do not grow on trees and so are impossible to find."

His grandmother did not answer him.

And after a moment he said softly,

"Grandpapa always claimed that you were the most beautiful woman he had ever seen and he fell in love with you the moment he entered the ballroom."

Lady Springdale gave him a watery smile.

"That is true. And your grandfather said to himself 'that is the girl I am going to marry', and he did marry me and we were very very happy together."

"When I walk into a ballroom and see the girl I am going to marry, I will let you know," her grandson said. "In fact I will bring her to you wherever you are and you will know that she was worth waiting for."

Lady Springdale sighed once more.

"You are a naughty boy," she said. "You always have a clever excuse for *not* doing what I want."

Her grandson laughed.

"Anyway I can see that you will soon be out of here and back in the house and looking after me as you always do when you are in London."

"I will indeed stay with you for a little while," she promised. "But you know how much they will miss me at home, especially my dogs and cats. I want to go back to the country as soon as I am well enough."

"Don't be in any hurry. I will come and see you tomorrow and you can tell me what the doctors have to say. After all you pay them enough and they might as well give you the information that I have always found difficult to coax out of them."

His grandmother laughed.

"That is true. But I expect I will do what I want to do and at the moment that is to be out of this hospital as quickly as possible, although I have to admit that they do look after me very well."

"And you must take things easy, Grandmama," he said, "as you often said to me, 'more haste, less speed'."

"You are a naughty boy and I become angry when you will not bring home a bride as I have been asking you to do for the last five years."

"I am sure it's much longer than that," her grandson replied. "But, when I do find her, I have a suspicion that you will say she is not good enough for me!"

"I will say nothing of the sort," Lady Springdale protested. "In fact I will be glad if you marry anyone, even if it is the kitchen maid!"

"You can be sure I will not do that," he answered. "I know very well how you disapprove of people who are not in the Royal Circle!"

"Now you are just making a mockery of the whole thing," Lady Springdale scolded him. "As I have told you already, all I want is for you to have a son to carry on the family and the title."

"There are a great number of women ready to take on my title," he replied and once again there was a note of sarcasm in his voice, "but I am looking for someone who is more interested in *me*."

"Who could fail to be interested in you, dear boy? Of course you are being modest, but I can count up on my fingers the ladies you have been attracted to these past five years, who unfortunately have already received a wedding ring before they met you!"

Lord Springdale rose to his feet.

"I am not going to argue with you, Grandmama, because you are far too clever and always have an answer to whatever I may say. What I do want you to do is to get well quickly. Otherwise I will worry about you and it's something I dislike doing."

"So you would let the women worry about you?" his grandmother retorted.

They both laughed.

He walked over to her bed and then bent down to his grandmother and kissed her on both cheeks.

"I will come back tomorrow, but if I cannot manage it, I will send you my love and excuses, Grandmama."

"There is only one excuse I should be pleased to have and that is that you are out with a very pretty girl who you found too enchanting to leave."

"I am not going to answer that," he replied as he walked towards the door. "Goodbye, Grandmama, and let me tell you that there are no girls around as pretty as you were at that age. In my humble opinion that is just what is wrong with the world."

He went out, closing the door behind him, before his grandmother could think of a suitable rejoinder.

She then lay back against her pillows thinking that if only he would be sensible about marriage, things would be very different.

In all her discussions with him, somehow he always managed to have the last word.

As her grandson was hurrying down the stairs to the front door of the hospital, she was praying as she had so often prayed before that he would fall in love, as his father and grandfather had done, and live happily ever afterwards.

*

Outside the hospital waiting for him was the chaise he had driven in from Berkeley Square to Chelsea.

When he appeared, the groom, who was holding the reins of the two horses, which were rather restless, climbed out of the driving seat and handed the reins to his Lordship.

As he did so, he pointed out,

"You forgot the flowers, my Lord, which we put in the back."

"Oh, so I did!" he exclaimed, "how stupid of me! Please take them in, Ben, and if there is no one to carry them upstairs, her Ladyship is on the first floor in the room on the left which looks over the river."

"I'll find it for sure, my Lord," Ben replied.

Picking up the bunch of spring flowers that Lord Springdale had bought on his way to Chelsea, Ben hurried into the hospital.

Holding the reins in his hands, Lord Springdale was now making himself comfortable in the driving seat when suddenly he was aware that someone had climbed into the chaise beside him and a woman's voice now said,

"Drive away – as quickly as you can!"

It was an order.

As he turned to look at the speaker, he saw that she was a young and very attractive girl.

As he gazed at her, she turned her head to look back at the entrance to the hospital with dread.

"Hurry! Hurry!" she cried. "We must get away as fast as we can."

Because the young girl was being so insistent, Lord Springdale, instead of arguing, did as she requested.

The horses were only too eager to oblige by moving as rapidly as possible down the road in front of him.

When they were some distance from the hospital, he turned to her and asked,

"Would you explain to me the reason for this speed and where do you want to go to?"

She looked at him and gave an exclamation as she replied,

"I am so sorry! I thought you were driving a hired vehicle – and I had to get away."

"What is frightening you?" Lord Springdale asked.

"Something most unpleasant," she answered, "and please, as you have been kind enough to take me away, would you stop as soon as we see a carriage I can hire."

"It would be easier," Lord Springdale replied, "if I take you where you want to go. Where is it, by the way?"

"Well, actually it is in Park Lane."

"As it happens," Lord Springdale told her, "I am going to Mayfair myself, so I will take you."

He thought, as Ben had been with him for so many years, he would not be in the least surprised in finding that he had disappeared when he returned to the chaise and he would take the easiest and doubtless the most comfortable way back to Berkeley Square.

"That is very kind of you," the girl answered, "and I am very sorry to be a nuisance."

"You are frightened," Lord Springdale asked, "so do tell me what has upset you?"

There was silence until the girl replied to him in a very different tone,

"I don't know if you have ever suffered in the way I have, but I swear that I will not marry anyone unless I fall in love first."

Lord Springdale turned his head to look at her in astonishment.

Then he laughed.

"You will not believe me," he said, "but I have just been saying the very same to my grandmother. I suspect that you have been pressured as I have been into marrying someone you do *not* wish to marry."

The girl stared at him.

"That is true and I refuse to marry any man who is after my money, but does not care one scrap about me."

She spoke violently as if she could not help herself.

Lord Springdale then smiled as he remarked,

"You put into words exactly what I am feeling."

"But then you are a man," the girl, whose name she told him was Mellina, replied. "Therefore you cannot be pressured, as I am, into marriage."

Lord Springdale thought to himself that he had had enough pressure put on him by his grandmother to last him for several years.

It was always the same story, he must marry and produce an heir.

He knew that she had really been frightened for a long time because, after he was born, his mother had been told by the doctors that it was impossible for her to have another child.

Of course he had been spoilt, he always admitted that himself.

But, just because they spoilt him as an only child, there was no reason that he could see why he should marry someone he was not the least in love with just because she might give him a son or perhaps if he was lucky two or three of them.

Because he was silent, Mellina remarked,

"It is difficult to explain to a man how a woman can be pushed, shoved and then literally thrown into a marriage simply because it is important for her to produce an heir."

"I know you will not believe me," Lord Springdale said, "but, as I am experiencing that at the moment, I can sympathise with you with all my heart."

"Can you really?" she quizzed him. "How funny, I really thought that it was only women who were forced into matrimony while the men always had it all their own way."

"I only wish that was true," he answered. "But tell me why you are being made to marry someone you don't want to."

He thought as he spoke that she would refuse to discuss it and least of all tell him the truth.

But after a moment's silence, Mellina said,

"I feel that I should tell you the truth because I have made use of you. The truth is that my father, who is in the hospital, is determined I should be married to someone he likes because he is so afraid that I will marry some ne'er-do-well fortune-hunter who will marry me for my father's money."

As she finished, she laughed somewhat ruefully and added,

"It does sound very complex when I say it. But as a stranger you might as well know the truth because I might not be free to say it again."

Lord Springdale was intrigued and declared,

"As I am in the same position as you, we should be honest with each other. Therefore I will tell you that I am being pressured into marriage because I have a title."

Mellina gazed at him and then after a moment she commented,

"I suppose I can understand that. All the girls I came out with are longing to marry a Duke or a Lord and I assume that would be some compensation. But my father, because he is convinced that the man I have danced with will throw all his precious money away, is determined that I should marry a man of *his* choice who I find utterly and completely repulsive."

She spoke almost violently.

Then, as Lord Springdale drove the horses towards Hyde Park, he said,

"It sounds terrifying. I am very sorry for you, but I suppose there is no escape."

"I managed to escape at the moment because my father has arranged that the man should meet with me at his bedside and take me back to our house where he intends to propose to me and I was told that I had to accept him."

"Surely your father cannot make you do that!" Lord Springdale exclaimed.

"You don't know my father. Although I am sure that you must have heard of him. I have always said that he is the most popular millionaire in London and everyone admires him because he is so rich."

"Then you must be talking of Mr. Weston," Lord Springdale said.

"I thought you would know his name," his daughter replied. "He fills all the columns in the Court Circular, because he has more money than anyone else."

"Then he is very lucky," Lord Springdale answered. "I should have thought that you are lucky too if you are his daughter."

"Lucky!" Mellina cried. "But I am pursued by men who are not a bit interested in me but my money. Now to protect me from those sorts of men my father has chosen the man I am to marry who, as I have just told you, I find totally repellent."

"Then you must definitely say so!" Lord Springdale suggested positively.

Mellina laughed, but there was no humour in it.

"Then you don't know my father. He always has his own way that is why he is so rich. He wins and he wins and he will win even if it kills me to marry this horrible man. In fact I would rather die than do so."

"Then you will have to run away," Lord Springdale declared.

She turned once again to look at him.

"I suppose that is what I am doing at the moment. Instead of going home – where can you take me where my father will not find me?"

"You know perfectly well that you cannot run away by yourself. You would then get yourself into all sorts of trouble and perhaps be very scared besides being robbed."

Lord Springdale paused before he went on,

"After all I suspect that the pearls round your neck are worth a fortune and your wristwatch is glittering every time you move your hands."

He meant his remark to be funny, but Mellina did not laugh.

Instead she insisted,

"I have to run away, I have to! I cannot bear that man, it makes me feel sick even to think of him. I know that Papa will force me to the altar and somehow the ring will be on my finger whatever I say and whatever I do now or later."

"It cannot be as bad as all that," Lord Springdale said.

"It is worse," she replied. "It is no use you trying to make it sound better. Just as my friends tell me that he is a very nice man and I have to make the best of it."

She gave an exclamation before she went on,

"*I* have to marry him, not them! I know I will kill myself rather than let him touch me."

"Surely," Lord Springdale said, "if you talk to your father and tell him that you feel like this, he will not make you do anything so distasteful and degrading."

"I know my father," Mellina replied. "If he makes up his mind he never changes it. That is why he is so rich, because he is so insistent he knows that he will win in the end."

"Then you will definitely have to run away. Where can you go?"

"That is what I am asking you," Mellina answered. "I have no relations who would hide me from Papa. In fact they are so terrified of not getting all the money he gives them, they would write at once and tell him I was there the moment I walked into one of their houses."

Lord Springdale thought that this was very likely true.

Then he enquired,

"There must be somewhere you can go."

"If there is, tell me about it?" she said. "After all, if someone is so persistent in forcing you to marry a man you dislike, there are not likely to be many hidey-holes waiting for one and that is exactly what my position is."

She gave a deep sigh before she continued,

"If I go home now, the man who Papa was waiting for will be sent to find me and however much I protest I will be forced eventually to marry him."

She was very obviously so unhappy and distraught by the thought that Lord Springdale felt extremely sorry for her.

He knew only too well that once relations made up their minds about anything that would save the family they would never stop forcing one into the unpleasant position of trying to escape them.

He knew only too well that his grandmother would tell her friends how stubborn he was being.

They would all rally themselves to try to force him into marriage so that no longer could she worry herself that if he had an accident there would be no one to take his place and the title.

"What can I do?" the girl beside him now asked desperately.

There was a note of such misery in her voice that he felt he must do something to help her.

"Under normal circumstances," he pointed out, "I would say that you must run to your closest friend or your nearest relations, but you tell me that suggestion would be fruitless."

"They would all then side with my Papa," Mellina explained, "in saying that the man he has chosen for me is a nice sensible man, who would appreciate and doubtless increase the huge amount of money I am inheriting from Papa and therefore, in their eyes, he would make a good husband for me."

She gave a little cry before she admitted,

"I have always believed that I would fall in love with someone who loved me because I was me, but now I know that will never happen. Never! Never! I will be unhappy, in fact miserable, for the rest of my life. I can only pray that it will not be a long one."

Lord Springdale reached the top of Sloane Street and then turned his horses into Hyde Park.

"I think that we should take a little fresh air by the Serpentine," he proposed, "and discuss all this as sensibly as we can."

He looked at her and smiled as he said,

"So then please don't try and drown yourself in the water as I have a new suit on!"

He meant to make her laugh and he succeeded.

"I promise you here and now that I will not try to drown myself in the Serpentine. Not today at any rate," she assured him.

"Then we will go where it is not crowded," Lord Springdale replied, "and find an answer to your problems."

"You can find an answer to yours by going away and the world is at your feet," Mellina answered. "But, as you have just told me, I cannot go alone and I am sensible enough to accept that that is the truth."

"Actually I had not thought of going away myself," Lord Springdale replied. "But it would certainly solve the problem at the moment. Perhaps, if I did go on a long trip, I might then find a woman I wanted to marry rather than be forced up the aisle, because my grandmother wants to be certain that the title will carry on and doubtless the bride would only be marrying me for my name."

He was really working it out for himself although he spoke lightly.

Mellina laughed before she pointed out,

"You are in a far better position than I am because you can choose the woman you marry while I have to take the man who has been selected for me by my father."

"As I have said," Lord Springdale repeated, "you will have to run away."

"But where and with whom?" she asked.

"I suppose, if I was a Cavalier, I would say with me," Lord Springdale replied.

"But, as you are not one, you will sit in London," Mellina said, "and look round at the hundreds of attractive young women who are just longing for a title and the lucky one will catch you."

Lord Springdale thought that she was clever enough to be speaking the truth.

Of course he would then be caught and pressed into matrimony by his grandmother and by the mother of the girl and doubtless her father would join in the undignified melee too.

He was well aware that it was not only his title that attracted the ambitious parents of a *debutante* or a girl they were frightened was going to be left on the shelf.

There were the girls themselves if they were young and pretty or expected that a Duke could fall down the chimney and beg them to marry him.

Or, if they were not quite so lucky, there would be someone of good standing.

It was those men who their mothers always invited to dinner every night and for weekends at their country houses when they could ride during the day and dance in the evening.

It was always expected that they would propose by the end of such a delightful weekend.

Lord Springdale had learnt very quickly once he left Oxford University that he was a Social catch.

There were undoubtedly a great number of mothers and daughters plotting to enslave him unless he was clever enough to realise danger almost before it appeared.

When he looked back, there had been a good few times when he had only managed at the very last moment to escape from what he had suddenly realised was a plot to ensnare him.

It was what his grandmother was plotting now.

He was quite certain that the moment she returned home from hospital he would be invited to several parties.

He would have to be very much aware that there was someone present who she considered would make him a good wife.

And he was absolutely certain that she would be a very dull and dismal one.

As he drove the horses up to the Serpentine and fastened the reins so that he did not have to hold them, he turned round in the driving seat to look at the girl next to him.

"Now we can talk," he said, "or rather plan your escape."

"I have just been thinking how hopeless it is," she answered. "Perhaps I should jump into the river and, if I was not able to swim, then I might sink into the mud and no longer be an attraction to fortune-hunters!"

"I think that is rather a messy way of dying," Lord Springdale remarked.

Then unexpectedly they both laughed.

"I know I sound ridiculous," Mellina said, "and you will suppose that I am imagining the direst circumstances more than is necessary."

She looked very serious as she went on,

"But for me it is a desperate one and I keep saying to myself I cannot marry that man, yet I know that no one will listen to me."

"I want to help you," Lord Springdale said. "If I was in the same position in a book I would have something sensible to say which would save us both."

"I have been lying awake at night and thought and thought," Mellina replied. "But there never seems to be a way out for me."

Lord Springdale reflected that he might almost say the same.

After all he knew that his grandmother would never cease trying to marry him off so that he could produce the heir she so wanted.

Because he was fond of her, in fact she was the one member of the family he really loved, he would doubtless give in simply because there was apparently no practicable alternative.

"You suggested I run away," Mellina said. "But I cannot think of anywhere I can go and I am sure that you are right in pointing out that it would be dangerous if I went alone."

"Of course it would," he nodded. "A young girl of your age, so pretty and apparently rich, would be a grave temptation to anyone. Even if you stayed in small hotels, there would still be men who would think you fair game."

"I have thought that out for myself," Mellina said. "Of course I could pay someone to go with me, but can you imagine anything worse than having to travel with servants and they would have to be women?"

She hesitated before she continued,

"I expect they would be seasick if we went abroad, while I would have no one to talk to."

Lord Springdale knew this was true and thought it was intelligent of her to work out the scenario for herself.

'What the devil can I do with the girl?' he asked himself.

It was not because he found her boring or tiresome, but because he was sincerely sorry for her.

21

Of course he had heard about her father's fortune, which was very much talked about in Society circles.

He remembered now that Mr. Weston's father was a gentleman by birth, who had gone away to explore the world as so many young men were anxious to do.

He had fallen on his feet in the most amazing way making vast profits on his ventures in the East, which was talked about with some awe.

He had then come back to England where he had married a very attractive woman, who was the daughter of an Earl.

They had produced a son and several daughters to the satisfaction of their grandfather.

It was in fact the son who had inherited his father's brains and he was born with the magic touch of turning everything he was interested in into gold.

He was, as it so happened, a man of considerable charm.

He was accepted Socially not only because of his money but because of his antecedents and the fact that he had never made anyone feel uncomfortable because he was so rich.

Now he thought about it, Lord Springdale felt that perhaps this girl was exaggerating her position.

Then he remembered his mother telling him that the family had somehow dispersed around the world.

The men the girls had married had either died from being soldiers or sailors or because they were continually abroad and had caught some of the nasty infections that were only found in foreign countries.

They had therefore not returned to England.

He could understand in a way that Mr. Weston was the end of a long run of family some of whom had spent their huge fortune in unnecessary and unrewarding ways.

Now he thought it out, the present Mr. Weston was the end of his family just as he was indeed the end of his own family.

That was why he was so anxious that his daughter should produce a suitable heir to inherit his great fortune.

In the meantime he would continue to increase it as long as she was producing grandchildren to whom he could leave it when he died.

This all passed through Lord Springdale's mind.

Then he looked once again at the girl beside him.

She was staring at the water of the Serpentine and he knew that, although the words had been spoken in jest, she had taken them seriously.

She was thinking that rather than marry the man she hated so much she was prepared to die.

"Now you have to be sensible about all this," Lord Springdale said.

"That is just what I am being," she answered. "But somehow I must run away, although where I can go I have no idea."

"As it so happens I have no idea where I can go either," Lord Springdale answered. "So I suggest, although it might seem extraordinary, that we go together!"

CHAPTER TWO

Mellina then turned round to look at him in sheer astonishment.

"What do you mean?" she asked.

"What I have just said," Lord Springdale replied. "Thinking it over, I should feel extremely lonely if I went off entirely on my own and you would feel the same."

He paused before he continued,

"What we are both seeking is love, the real love that we have always believed in but could never find."

Melina stared at him in surprise.

"Of course you are right," she said. "Ever since I was old enough to read I thought that the love I read about in books was something I would find myself when I was grown up."

"Many men must have already told you that they love you," Lord Springdale said a little sarcastically.

Mellina shook her head.

"No, not really," she replied. "They have paid me compliments and made a big fuss of me, but I knew all the time that they were thinking about Papa's money."

She was silent for a moment.

Then she went on,

"I suppose just as no one can think of you without remembering you have a title, no one looks at me without realising that I am sitting on thousands and thousands of pieces of gold!"

Lord Springdale laughed.

"It sounds a bit funny, but honestly I am really very sympathetic and understanding. Therefore I would suggest that we make it an adventure and we try to find, each for ourselves, the real love that you have read about and I have thought about ever since I was old enough to do so."

"It would be wonderful if we could really find it," Mellina said in a low voice. "I want someone to feel that he would love me even if I did not have a single penny."

"And I want someone to love me if I had no title, but was just plain Mr. Jones," Lord Springdale added.

Mellina laughed.

"I cannot quite imagine you as that. But I can well understand in a way that the title glorifies you to an extent that they think of the prestige rather than of you."

"Of course they do," Lord Springdale agreed, "and it's so irritating. Therefore shall we set out on an adventure to find the love we are both looking for, but so far have not been able to find?"

There was silence while Mellina turned over in her mind what he had just said.

Then she asked a little cautiously,

"Can we really do it?"

"I can certainly," he answered, "but your father will be frantic if you just disappear."

There was more silence while she was thinking.

Then she said,

"I could write him a letter saying I was so upset that he wants to force me into marriage with a man I actively dislike that I have gone away to stay with friends and to think over what he has said to me and what I must do in the future."

"You don't think he will send the Police to look for you?"

Mellina shook her head.

"Papa would hate any publicity concerning me or his money," she replied. "Therefore he would never go to the Police unless he thought that I had been killed or taken prisoner. Even then he would not want it to appear in the newspapers."

Lord Springdale laughed.

"That is what we all think. I wince when I see they have mentioned me at some particular party and inferred that I was courting the young woman it was given for."

"That must often happen to you," Mellina said, "so I can quite understand why you would want to run away too."

"Well it will be an adventure and give those who are bullying us time to settle down and think that they must be kinder and more respectful of us in the future."

"That is exactly what I want," Mellina agreed, "but my father is obsessed by money and believes that it is more important than anything else in the world."

"I admit it has some relevance," Lord Springdale observed, "and I have no wish to be penniless. At the same time you and I are looking for something quite different."

"Yes," Mellina replied. "We are looking for love, *real* love. The love that men and women have fought for and died for since the beginning of time."

Lord Springdale sighed,

"Perhaps we will never find it."

"But at least we will have tried," she murmured.

"And this then is a unique opportunity that makes it easy," he declared, "because we both have a real reason for going into hiding."

There was silence for a moment and then Mellina remarked,

"I am sure Papa will be furious. But I cannot help feeling that he will keep quiet about it because he would not like his friends to know that he had driven me away because he was forcing me to marry a man I had no wish to marry."

"That puts it all into a nutshell!" Lord Springdale exclaimed. "My grandmother has bullied me until I begin to feel sick if anyone should mention the dreaded word 'marriage'."

"Now how shall I do it?" Mellina asked. "If I go now and collect my clothes, I can leave the house before Papa comes back from the hospital. They talked about him coming home tomorrow or the next day."

"That makes it very much easier," Lord Springdale replied. "My yacht is anchored off the Embankment and that is the way we can leave London without anyone being aware of it."

"You have a yacht? How wonderful! But I think it would be wise to go aboard your yacht after dark," Mellina suggested, "so that no one will see us."

"Yes, of course," he agreed. "I am just wondering how I should explain your presence to the Captain."

As she did not answer, he went on,

"You must realise that, if it is known that you are travelling alone with me, it will damage your reputation and then your father will undoubtedly insist that I marry you even though I have no wish to do so."

He paused before he continued,

"Or else you will be forced up the aisle as quickly as possible with the man he has already chosen as your husband."

Mellina considered his words.

And then she said,

"Perhaps I am wrong, but everyone would surely be suspicious of someone you took with you unless she was a relative."

"But of course they would," he replied. "Therefore, to solve the problem, I will say that you are my sister. As I travel without a title, no one could look you up in *Debrett's Peerage* and claim that I don't have one!"

"Perhaps we should think of a name for ourselves which no one will think significant or distinctive," Mellina said.

She smiled before she continued,

"At the same time you will have to remember that we are travelling in a yacht, which will make them certain that we at least have money to spend on such a luxury."

"You are quite right," he agreed. "But, if we go to the places that I have in mind, we can leave the yacht in Port and travel as the locals do. Personally I much prefer a horse."

"So do I," Mellina enthused. "So I will remember to pack my riding habit whatever else I leave behind."

"What I think you have to do," he continued, "is to consider that we don't want to cause too much interest. But you have to look pretty to attract the man who may eventually be the one you are seeking and I have to do the same where women are concerned."

"That is common sense," Mellina said approvingly. "So what you are saying is that I will require my pretty clothes as well as my plain ones."

"If I had a sister, which I have not," he said, "she would always look pretty and smart just as my mother did when she was alive."

Mellina looked thoughtful and then she said,

"We must think of a name which is not too dull just in case anyone bothers about us even though we are not trying to attract any attention."

"What do you suggest?" Lord Springdale enquired.

Mellina thought over a number of names before she said,

"What about 'Blakeley'?"

As he was thinking it over, Lord Springdale moved his horses away from the Serpentine because too many people were circling round them.

After they had driven a little way in silence, Lord Springdale said,

"I see nothing wrong with the name 'Blakeley'. It does not resemble either of our names in any way."

"Then it is 'the Blakeleys' we should be!" Mellina exclaimed. "And I think that because you are so tall and handsome you should be 'Colonel Blakeley', who served in the Grenadier Guards for several years."

Lord Springdale laughed.

"That does sound very romantic, only unfortunately I do not have the right uniform."

"You have left it at home as you have now retired owing to the fact that you have to look after your family estate," Mellina suggested.

"You are obviously making me the sort of fanciful hero I would want to be," Lord Springdale replied, "but what about you?"

There was silence while she ruminated about it.

Then he said,

"I think you are too modest to say so, but I can. We say that you have had so many men placing their hearts at your feet that you have had to come away with me to stop thinking about love and marriage, but instead the world in general."

He paused before he added,

"They must not for a moment think that you had an unfortunate love affair, but just that you are tired of being pursued by so many young admirers who all want to marry you because you are so attractive."

Mellina smiled.

"I do wish that was true, but actually I have only had two rather feeble offers of marriage unless you count Papa's man, who has not communicated his desire for my money to me, but merely agreed with Papa that I would have a very nice trousseau."

Lord Springdale laughed.

As he did so, he realised that he was near her house in Park Lane.

He was aware at once that it was one of the largest and most impressive houses that overlooked Hyde Park.

He had not had to ask her where she was going, because, although he had not said so, he had met her father at a ball he had once attended.

Mr. Weston had asked him if he would like to dine with him one night and added where he lived.

"Now here you are," he said. "As your father is not at home, you have plenty of time to pack and I will collect you at nine o'clock when it is getting dark and we will go straight down to the mooring where my yacht is anchored on the River Thames."

As he spoke, he then drew in his horses outside her house.

The front door opened immediately and he realised that the butler was looking out to see who was calling.

"Be very careful what you say," Lord Springdale warned. "If you change your mind, just send a letter to number 10 Berkeley Square which is my address."

"I promise you most sincerely that I will not change my mind," Mellina assured him.

She climbed out of the carriage.

Lord Springdale watched her walk up the steps of the house until, when she reached the front door, she then turned round.

He raised his hat and drove off.

He was thinking as he did so that this was certainly an adventure.

All his life he had enjoyed his adventures although they had been, at times, more disastrous than he liked to remember.

And what he was intending to do now struck him as something more extreme and exciting than anything he had ever done before.

And he would doubtless become very bored with the girl.

But she would be someone to talk to for the first two or three days, although doubtless she would succumb to seasickness when they reached the Bay of Biscay and would have to remain in her cabin.

'I expect,' he thought to himself as he walked up the stairs of his house, 'I will come back exactly as I am at the moment. Unmarried and fighting to free myself from the women who Grandmama will have accumulated during my absence. She will still be convinced once again that I will take one of them as my future wife.'

His valet was quite unmoved when he told him that he was going to visit some fiends on the Continent and he required sufficient clothes for perhaps two weeks or even a month.

"I'll have them ready in an hour or two, my Lord," the valet promised and hurried off to bring his cases down from the attic.

Lord Springdale went to his study where there was a pile of letters waiting for him on the writing desk.

He knew without looking at them that there would be endless invitations to the parties that were being given every night.

They were either for a *debutante* or else, which he much preferred, married couples, every one of whom flirted outrageously with each other and him.

At the same time amusingly, so that he was never bored in their company.

'Perhaps I would have been wiser,' he thought to himself, 'if I had taken a married woman with me.'

But that would have been impossible.

No one, however indifferent he was to his wife, would allow her to travel round the Continent alone with anyone like Lord Springdale.

He was well aware that he had acquired what his grandmother thought was a somewhat bad character where women were concerned.

Equally he had never deliberately seduced a woman away from her husband.

In fact they had invariably thrown themselves into his arms even before he was ready for them to do so.

Now he thought about it, it was really rather sad that, after so many years in London, he could honestly say that there was not one woman he minded leaving behind him.

Nor was there any woman he longed to see again when he was not with her.

'I suppose,' he said to himself as he sat down at his desk, 'the trouble is I am spoilt and so independent that I am quite content to be alone. I am really the sort of man who should never marry.'

But he could not help hoping that perhaps this visit to the world outside would be different from the others he had undertaken.

He had enjoyed himself at times. Of course he had.

But he had always been thankful to return home.

He loved being in the country with his horses and his estate.

But what it really amounted to was the fact that he found it hard to be unkind to his grandmother and the other members of the family who invariably kept pressing him to be married and produce the elusive heir.

'I should have shut them up,' he then told himself, 'when they first started. Now even if I swore at them they would not listen to me.'

In fact the only solution at the moment was to go abroad and search for what he could not find in England.

And that was love!

*

At her home Mellina was finding it more difficult than Lord Springdale was to getting ready to go away.

First of all her lady's maid kept asking her what she was doing, where she was going to and if she would meet anyone of particular importance where she was staying.

"I have no idea until I arrive," Mellina replied.

"But you will want your best dresses," the lady's maid insisted.

"Of course I will," Mellina answered. "I will also want my swimming suit and riding clothes."

"Now I think that I can guess, miss, where you be goin'," the lady's maid said. "If they have 'orses, I be sure it be with your father's friends in Sussex."

Because she thought it would be the right thing to say, Mellina told her,

"I may drop in there on my way home. Certainly their horses are more impressive than any of the others I have seen."

"Then you must take your best and newest ridin' clothes," the lady's maid prattled on. "I will pack them at the bottom of your trunk. What do you think you will want for tomorrow or the next day, miss?"

It was difficult to keep her quiet.

Somehow Mellina managed to answer all her lady's maid's questions without her being over-curious or more suspicious that she was not actually going to the place she mentioned.

Leaving her bedroom, Mellina went downstairs into the large and imposing drawing room that her father filled with people whenever he gave a party.

Because he was so rich he could afford to give his friends the very best food and the finest wines that could be found anywhere.

He also arranged if they were dancing the cotillion to give those who took part in it delightful and usually very extravagant presents.

For the ladies who particularly pleased him there was always a bouquet to take home with them when they left or a large box of chocolates that came from the most expensive shop in Bond Street.

It was rather sad, Mellina reflected, that she had never really enjoyed those parties.

This was because she was always suspicious of the men she sat next to at dinner or the men her father brought up to dance with her.

She knew almost by the way he introduced them and the cheery way he made them welcome that they were prospective husbands for her.

'I hate them, I hate them all,' she said to herself as she gazed round the large room. 'If I eventually do find a wonderful man, as his Lordship thinks I will, it will be a miracle.'

She then sat down at the writing desk and wrote a letter to her father.

She told him that she was tired of London and was therefore going to stay with some friends in the country.

"*They are talking about going over to France for a weekend,*" she wrote, "*and I will enjoy that.*

So please don't worry if you don't hear from me as it means I will be abroad and you know how tiresome they can be about the post."

Because she was so anxious to get away, she was ready long before there was any chance of Lord Springdale calling for her.

She ate a quick meal in the dining room.

Then she went into the music room to play a rather dismal piece of music that she had bought by mistake.

She had thought it was gay and the sort of music that one could dance to.

But instead it was a rather formal and exceedingly gloomy concerto.

'Perhaps I am mad to be doing this,' she thought to herself. 'Perhaps Lord Springdale will change his mind at the last moment and not come to collect me. After all he made it obvious I do not attract him and, if he does find the beautiful woman he is searching for, I will be sent home alone.'

Then she told herself she was being unnecessarily pessimistic about what was surely an exciting, unusual and extremely strange adventure for any girl to even think of undertaking.

After all she had never met Lord Springdale before today, although she had glimpsed him at several parties.

Her father's friends would think that she was mad to go off in this wild manner with a man she knew nothing about.

She would undoubtedly lose her reputation if she was not circumspect on his yacht and she would be a cast-off from Society if it was known what she was doing.

Her father would have a stroke if he was aware of it.

What was more, if her escapade was brought into the light of day, her father would insist on Lord Springdale marrying her to save her reputation and he would therefore hate her for the rest of their lives together.

'Maybe I should stay here and just tell Papa that I will most definitely not marry the man who he has chosen for me,' she thought.

Even as the idea came to her, she remembered just how much he repulsed her and how the mere thought of him touching her would make her scream hysterically.

'I hate him! I hate him!' she repeated to herself realising that she was now stamping her foot on the thick Aubusson carpet.

Then she told herself,

'If I stay here, as I ought to do, there is no doubt that Papa will somehow, by some trick or other, marry me off to the man I hate and I will be utterly and completely miserable.'

Surely it was better to take the risk of going with Lord Springdale, who had made it quite clear that she did not attract him in any way.

He was just glad to have her company on what for him was a wild adventure to find the wife he was being cajoled into taking.

'When he does find her,' Mellina thought, 'he will want me to help him. Maybe I will have to tell the woman or girl how charming he is or perhaps she will fall in love with him at first sight and will ask me to help her.'

It all seemed rather a muddle.

At the same time she recognised that she was taking a great risk in going off with a stranger even though he was from a respected and well known family.

Because she was feeling so worried, she walked up and down the room thinking that somehow she must keep moving.

'I cannot do this,' one side of her kept saying.

'And if you don't do it,' the other side then came in, 'you will find yourself up the aisle with your father rubbing his hands together in glee.'

She sighed.

'You will be forced to remain for the rest of your life,' she went on telling herself, 'with a man you hate and despise. Anything, however peculiar, however frightening, is better than that prospect.'

She then had to admit to herself that, although she thought him rather strange, Lord Springdale made her feel that his proposition for them was not only exciting but also a sensible escape from what was wrong and intimidating.

'He has asked me to join him as a companion and not as a woman,' she told herself, 'and certainly not a very attractive one. That in itself makes me feel sure that I will not be frightened.'

Then she had a sudden idea.

One essential matter she had not thought about was money.

As, if she wanted to escape from Lord Springdale, it was important that she should have the money to do so.

She knew where her father always kept a certain amount of cash in his bedroom.

This was because, if he needed it in a hurry, it was easier for him to have it on hand than to send his secretary to open the safe in his office.

So she ran up the stairs to her father's bedroom and was relieved to find that his valet was not there.

She knew the secret place where he kept the key.

Taking it in her hand, she walked to the safe in the wall, which her father had built there soon after he bought the house.

It only took Mellina a few minutes to open the safe and to find, as she expected, a great number of notes from the largest to the smallest, also quite a considerable amount of golden guineas.

She picked up a handful of coins and then counted out fifty five pound notes.

She felt that these would surely bring her home in comfort. Or alternatively she could buy anything that she required while they were travelling.

She had also seen her lady's maid put her cheque book into her trunk.

She knew now with some satisfaction that she was independent, if she wanted to be, of Lord Springdale.

She would be able not only to come home at any moment if she wished to do so but also pay for someone to travel with her and protect her from anything that might hurt or disturb her.

'I am now thinking sensibly,' she told herself, 'as if I am older than I am. Perhaps this is help from Heaven, because I am quite certain when Papa finds out that I have gone and has no idea where I am, he will not terrify me another time as he has done today.'

It was exactly at nine o'clock, when, having put on a warm coat to travel in and a small veil over her head, Mellina, waiting at the top of the stairs, heard a knock on the front door.

She ran down the stairs at the same moment as the butler opened the door and she found herself facing Lord Springdale.

"Good evening, Mellina," he began. "You are very punctual and that is a good thing as our friends are waiting for us and I really don't want to start the journey by being late."

She realised that he was speaking in this way to impress the butler.

"No, of course not," Mellina replied. "I only hope that I have not brought too much luggage with me."

"Oh, there will be plenty of room in the carriage," Lord Springdale replied casually. "I am sure your servants will put it in the back. Let me help you down the steps. It is very dark tonight and there is no moon."

He took her hand as he spoke.

She knew from the pressure of his fingers that he was pleased with her appearance and the way they were leaving without anyone to say goodbye to or to ask where they were actually going.

In fact as the carriage door was closed by a footman and the horses started off down Park Lane, Mellina gave a little cry of delight,

"We have done it! We have done it! We have got away without anyone bothering us or having the slightest idea where we are going."

"That is just what I hoped you would say," Lord Springdale replied. "The yacht, on my instructions, has moved nearer to the Houses of Parliament and the sooner we set sail the better."

"That is what I was thinking," Mellina enthused. "It is all a very exciting adventure for me and I hope for you too."

"Whether it is a successful one, we will only know when we return," he said with some complacency. "I do not mind betting you will find what you are seeking long before I do!"

Mellina laughed.

"I was thinking the same thing. I was just going to say I am certain that you will be successful while I will come home empty-handed."

"We may, however, both fail in our endeavour to find someone remarkable," Lord Springdale said, "and then we can cry on each other's shoulders."

He paused before he continued,

"But I want to be optimistic and think that we will both succeed and I will dance at your wedding and you can dance at mine!"

"I only hope that is the truth and not just a fantasy," Mellina remarked.

For a moment they drove on in silence.

She was thinking as they did so that she was sure that no one else she had ever known would have been as brave as she was being.

She only hoped that her father, at the last moment, would do nothing to prevent her from leaving England.

Sitting beside her, Lord Springdale was aware of the sweetness of the scent she was wearing.

He thought to himself she was in fact very brave to do anything so Socially outrageous as to set off alone and un-chaperoned with a man she had just met.

'She certainly has guts,' he now thought to himself. 'Although it is hardly something one wants in a woman, even though it is essential in a man.'

At the same time, as this adventure was so original and so far at any rate had not fallen to pieces, he believed optimistically it might eventually turn out to be successful.

He thought as he drove from his house to Park Lane that he would not have been at all surprised if at the last moment Mellina had backed out and said that she could not accompany him after all.

And she would doubtless have a very good reason for doing so.

The real reason that she could not travel alone with a strange man she had only just met would be brushed on one side.

Yet she was here and apparently prepared to play the part of pretending to be his sister while they searched the world to find the love they were both seeking.

'I would not have taken a bet about this happening even after we had talked about it,' Lord Springdale thought as they passed Buckingham Palace at speed and were now proceeding towards the Embankment.

Then, as he had the first glimpse of Big Ben and the House of Commons, he thought that it was indeed a superb adventure and if it failed there would be no regrets.

But if it succeeded both he and Mellina would be able to congratulate themselves for the rest of their lives.

'All I can say,' he thought as they drew nearer and nearer to his yacht, 'is that we are undoubtedly gambling on an uncertainty and it would be an absolute wonder if it came off.'

It was then to his surprise, as the horses turned the corner onto the Embankment, he felt Mellina slip her hand into his.

"This is very exciting," she said in a low voice. "I am going to pray that we will both win what at the moment seems an almost impossible race into the unknown."

"We just have to win," Lord Springdale told her, "because I am too proud to go back and admit that I am a failure."

Mellina laughed and took her hand from his.

"It would not be you who is the failure," she said, "but the woman you meet who fails to attract you as she ought to do."

Lord Springdale laughed.

"That is one way of looking at it. If we are too serious about this, we will frighten people away. We have to see the funny side of it all, at least, when we two are together."

"But it is funny," Mellina answered. "Equally I am terrified that Papa might be suspicious and send someone to find out where I am going."

"I hope that you have not told anyone the truth," Lord Springdale quizzed her.

"No, of course not," Mellina replied. "I have made it very clear that I was moving about with my friends from place to place and so could give no particular address for Papa or anyone else to find me."

"That sounds sensible. One thing they will never imagine in their wildest dreams is that you are with me."

"We must go well away from England and discover new places," Mellina said, "where no one has the slightest idea who we are and are not that interested anyway."

"I agree with you," Lord Springdale smiled. "But I think we should start by having a look at the French. After all they know a great deal about love and if we look around I am sure we will find amusing and interesting people who would be happy to welcome us as foreigners."

He laughed as he went on,

"Then you will find that the men would pay you every possible compliment you would ever want to hear."

"I have met quite a few Frenchmen with my Papa," Mellina told him. "They are very good at saying the right thing, kissing one's hand and paying one very elaborate compliments, but I have always suspected, and I am sure you have too, that to them it is all part of a game and they don't mean a word of it."

Lord Springdale threw back his head and laughed.

"You have described them precisely," he said. "I have always thought that French women are as insincere as the men. They not only take compliments very cleverly but give them. By the way they look at one and the soft touch of their hands makes you believe they are completely sincere in finding you different from anyone they have met before and certainly more attractive."

It was Mellina's turn to laugh and she did so.

"I had a French friend when I was at school," she said, "and you have described exactly how she always got her own way."

She paused before she went on,

"She was so clever that even all the teachers were taken in by her. She used to pay them compliments and make herself charming when she wanted to do something they did not want her to do – and she always won."

"As she won with the teachers, so she will win with every man she meets," Lord Springdale said. "Therefore I promise you that I will not believe one word I hear from the French women we will meet in France. But you have to be sensible and realise that the same applies to the men as well."

"I think what you are really saying," she answered, "is that we must look after each other and so make quite certain that we are not taken in or deceived in any way."

Lord Springdale then thought that that would apply more to Mellina than to himself.

Equally he was surprised and rather amused by the fact that she was not the rather simple girl she appeared to be, but was clever enough to look below the surface and judge people not by what they said but by what they were.

'I suppose,' he said to himself as the carriage came to a halt, 'I will learn something I have not learnt before on this voyage just as Mellina will learn that the world is not what she expects it to be.'

Lord Springdale climbed out of the carriage first.

As he took Mellina's hand in his to help her to the ground, he said,

"Welcome aboard and may we both find our way to El Dorado!"

CHAPTER THREE

The yacht was even more impressive than Mellina had expected.

She had actually seen a number of yachts when her father had taken her with him when he had bought one for himself.

Yachts had become very popular in England.

The smartest young men-about-town thought that it increased their status when, as well as magnificent horses, they had a yacht that they could take to sea.

Lord Springdale himself had travelled a great deal after he bought his yacht when he was only twenty-one.

His father had said it was a necessary extravagance.

But he knew that he wanted it at first because it was very smart to have one and then because he realised that it was a place he could escape to away from the pressure put on him by his family.

He had therefore often slipped away before they could stop him to visit a great number of places overseas.

He found them not only fascinating but they taught him a great deal.

He thought now as they went aboard that perhaps he had made a silly mistake in saying that they would go to Paris.

He knew Paris so well.

And he knew too that a number of people would be waiting to welcome him once he arrived.

In fact they would only be exchanging the gaieties of London for the gaieties of Paris.

What was more they would then have to give up the yacht and travel to Paris by train.

'It was stupid of me to think of going there,' Lord Springdale now scolded himself.

As they stepped aboard the yacht, he was piped, as was correct, by two members of the crew.

The Captain then came running along to welcome them once they had set foot on the deck.

"I wish to speak to you alone," Lord Springdale said after he had shaken hands with the Captain. "But first I would like to introduce you to my sister, Mellina, who is coming with me."

The Captain bowed over her hand.

They walked into the Saloon and sat down on the comfortable sofas, which were covered with a green satin, the colour of the sea.

"Do sit down, Captain," Lord Springdale said. "I have something I want to talk to you about as I need your help."

"Which I am very willing to give your Lordship," the Captain replied politely.

"My sister and I," Lord Springdale began, "are now running away from the festivities of London and the fact that we have too many people pressing us to do what we have no wish to do, the majority of whom will not take no for an answer."

The Captain nodded as if he understood.

Then Lord Springdale went on,

"I know we have a new crew on board and so there is no reason for them to know anything about me or my sister. As you know when I have travelled with you before I have always changed my name and forgotten my title."

"That's true enough, my Lord," the Captain replied. "But I often think it's somewhat dangerous."

"And why should you think that?" Lord Springdale asked curiously.

"Because, my Lord, in many ways the fact that you are so important in England protects you abroad. There are those who would take what they could off any traveller, but they would be far too nervous to cheat or insult an English gentleman, who also bore an ancient title."

"I see your point," Lord Springdale said. "That is why I have, on certain occasions, called myself just 'Mr.' and escaped from, if nothing else, the newspapers."

The Captain laughed.

"That's true. But if your Lordship remembers, the last time you came aboard we went to places we had never been to before, some of which I hope we never have to go to again!"

"I agree with you, Captain, but for the moment let's forget them and concentrate on this escapade we need your help over."

He hesitated for a moment before he went on,

"To be frank my sister is escaping from a man who is determined to marry her and then I am escaping a certain crowd who prevent me from enjoying myself the way I wish to."

"I do understand, my Lord," the Captain answered. "Have you thought of a name to use so that no one will be waiting to interview you as soon as we arrive at a Port?"

This had happened several times on the last voyage and his Lordship had faced great difficulties in disguising himself and keeping the local newspapers from knowing who he really was.

Of course such a magnificent yacht attracted very considerable attention wherever it sailed.

When he wanted to be anonymous it was extremely annoying to be interviewed.

He was aware on several occasions that, if the men had discovered who he actually was, there was no doubt they would have sent a message to the London newspapers and hoped to be paid for doing so.

"Now, Captain, as far as the crew is concerned, I thought a good name would be 'Blakeley'. Mr. and Miss Blakeley and my sister's Christian name, as you already know is 'Mellina'. But there is no reason for them to use it."

"No, of course not, my Lord," the Captain agreed.

"So from now on," Lord Springdale continued, "we are just 'Mr. Blakeley' and 'Miss Blakeley' and I am very anxious that no one should know where we are going or who we are."

"I'll certainly do my best," the Captain promised.

"I thought that we would start with Gibraltar," Lord Springdale went on, "and from there we will go down the North coast of Africa, which is something I have not done for a very long time."

"Not in my time, my Lord," the Captain remarked.

"We will start off at once, Captain, and we can only hope that the sea is pleasant to us in the Bay of Biscay. I have warned my sister that she will doubtless spend most of the time in her bed. But it will be calm enough in the Mediterranean and I am sure that she will enjoy being with you and escaping, as we both are, from the gaieties and exhaustion of London."

"I will do my best," the Captain replied, "to make your Lordship and your sister comfortable and from this moment I will remember that you are Mr. Blakeley and Miss Mellina Blakeley."

He rose as he spoke and bowed to them both.

Then, opening the door, he left the Saloon.

Mellina, who had not said a word while they were talking, smiled at Lord Springdale.

"And from now on," she said, "I must remember that you are 'Ian' and I refer to you as 'my brother'."

"I only hope that I will make you a good one," he replied. "Quite frankly I think it is very brave of you to run away like this."

"The alternative being to drown myself rather than marry that ghastly man. But, as I am a good swimmer, I am certain that I would only end up on the other side of the Thames!"

Lord Springdale laughed.

"That would be an anticlimax," he said. "I suggest that from this moment you forget that man's existence, also your father's undoubted disappointment and I will forget my grandmother's."

Mellina clapped her hands together.

"We are doing it! We are actually doing what you suggested!" she exclaimed. "To me it is the most thrilling and exciting thing I have ever done in my whole life."

Lord Springdale smiled.

"Let's hope we will come home triumphant as we mean to do," he replied. "But let's be honest and say it is not an easy task we have set ourselves."

"No, of course not," Mellina agreed. "But to me it is very wonderful that you, Ian, a complete stranger, have been kind enough to help me escape and have invited me to join you on this wonderful yacht. Please can I see more of it?"

"You shall see it all. I think first it would be a good idea for you to choose your cabin from quite a selection of them."

Mellina clapped her hands again.

"Oh, let's do that!" she exclaimed. "As you have already said you expect me to spend a great deal of time in my cabin, so I would like one that is not only comfortable but pretty."

"All my cabins are superb," he said boastfully, "but you must appreciate it that I cannot give you the Master cabin as I would do if you were a very important female guest. That is mine, as I am the owner of this yacht, and you, as my sister, must I am afraid take second best."

"That is just what I would expect anyway," Mellina replied with a little smile.

Lord Springdale realised at once that she was rather surprised at the suggestion that she would want the Master cabin.

It was certainly what any other lady would have expected if he had taken her aboard.

And he suspected that she did not realise it was the one cabin that boasted a large double bed.

While all the rest were comfortable berths for one person.

The yacht was now moving slowly into the centre of the Thames.

As it did so, Lord Springdale and Mellina walked down the companionway and along the passage on either side of which were the cabins.

It was when they reached the end, which was the door into the Master cabin, that Lord Springdale opened a door into a cabin on the right of it, saying as he did so,

"I think that this is the most comfortable cabin and certainly the prettiest."

Mellina then followed him through the open door and gave a cry of surprise.

The cabin was in soft pink.

The curtains, which were made of pink chintz, had bunches of roses and honeysuckle on them.

The berth had curtains of pink chiffon edged with silver.

When he had the yacht built, Lord Springdale had been enamoured of a very attractive lady.

Pink had been her favourite colour because it was a perfect background for her fair hair and dazzling white skin.

She was, of course, married, but her husband was conveniently away on business in America and so she had spent the first month of his absence with Lord Springdale.

He thought now how ardently he had endeavoured to make her really comfortable and enjoy the journey.

It was only when they were going home that he had found himself thinking with satisfaction of his horses in the country and having a sudden urge to be alone.

In fact he thought to himself as they both stepped ashore from the yacht,

'Enough is enough and it is time I faced the truth.'

However, as he expected, Mellina was thrilled with the cabin.

"It is lovely! Simply lovely!" she exclaimed with delight. "If I have to retire here because I am a bad sailor, I will most certainly enjoy every moment of being confined to somewhere so pretty."

Lord Springdale then showed her his cabin.

Mellina was duly impressed with the large double bed and the neatly fitted furniture which made it seem even bigger than it actually was.

She could not resist going to one of the portholes to gaze out excitedly at the other side of the Thames as they were passing by.

They were by now well into the middle of the river where there was a strong tide running down to the sea.

"How can I be so lucky, so incredibly lucky," she asked, "to have met you? Now we are travelling away from all our troubles and exploring the world, which will be different from anything we have ever attempted before."

Lord Springdale did not spoil what she was saying by telling her that he had actually run away previously several times since he had purchased the yacht.

He wondered if any of his friends would believe that this time he was with a girl he had only just met, who was very different in every way from the beautiful ladies who had accompanied him in the past.

"What we have to plan," he said, "is where we will go that will be different from anywhere I have been before. As I am very keen to see a little of the South side of the Mediterranean, I think it will turn out to be quite different from anything we will find on the North side."

"It would be fun to visit Marseilles," Mellina said suddenly. "I was reading about it the other day and they are deliberately trying to make it attractive so that people would not always go to Paris, but find Marseilles, which can be reached by ship, is an equal attraction."

"I see their point," Lord Springdale replied. "And, of course, it has an excellent harbour. I will speak to the Captain about it and we might just stop there before we cross to the other side of the Mediterranean."

"Anywhere we go will be new and exciting to me," Mellina said. "But rather than miss anything, I hope that you will tell me what you have read or what you have seen already of the places we will visit. It would be sad to miss the chance of seeing something fascinating."

Lord Springdale did not like to say that on some of his trips he had been so obsessed by the lady with him that the history of where they had visited or the town they had seen had made very little impression on him.

"You will not be surprised to find out that I have a library on board," he told her. "In fact one cabin is filled with books. So you will be able to look up for yourself and read what is essential for us to view before we pass on to our next Port of call."

Mellina stared at him.

"You are wonderful!" she cried. "I have never met a man who read anything but the business columns of the newspapers!"

"So I must be the exception," he replied, "although naturally you have read the Court columns and reports of the previous night's parties every day!"

"I am not going to answer that," Mellina told him. "Instead I am going to beg you to show me your books."

Lord Springdale laughed as he opened a cabin door on the other side of the yacht.

When she went in, Mellina gave a cry of delight.

There were many shelves of books reaching from the floor to the ceiling.

Nearly all of them she could see at a glance were history or guide books.

"How could you be so sensible as to have arranged this cabin as well as all the others?" she asked. "I am sure that everyone you entertained as a guest has been grateful to you for feeding their brains as well as their bodies and, of course, their eyes."

Lord Springdale laughed again.

"Most of them were quite content with the comforts of the flesh and, if you read all these books before we reach home, you will certainly be exceptional."

"I will try," Mellina said, "and, if I am reading, I will not be able to bore you by asking you question after question about the places we visit. That, I am sure, you would find exceptionally dreary."

Lord Springdale thought that on previous occasions women had only wanted him to talk about themselves and for him to pay them endless compliments.

He could not recall anyone who would have taken what he called, 'my library', at all seriously.

Mellina had by now selected two books from the shelves and put them under her arm.

"Firstly I am going to read all about Gibraltar as I heard you telling the Captain to stop there. After that you will have to tell me where we are going so that I am well acquainted with the geography of the place before we even arrive there."

"What do you think I will be doing if you are so immersed in my library that you have no time for me?" he questioned.

Mellina chuckled.

"I promise you, Ian, that I will always have time for you. I am not only grateful to you for bringing me here, but I am also interested in you as a person."

She added quickly as though he did not understand,

"I often think that we take people for granted. To us they are just a man or a woman, while they themselves are original and unusual and, although we are sometimes not aware of it, either virtuous like an angel from Heaven or a devil from Hell itself!"

"That is something I have never thought about, but it is obviously a subject we will discuss at the dinner table, Mellina, if you are not too busy reading for the rest of the day to talk to me!"

"Now you are being absurd. Of course I want to talk to you. I feel I will learn more from you than anyone else I have ever met. At the same time I don't want to bore you or for you to wish the journey had come to an early end simply because I had talked too much as women often do."

"That is true enough," he replied. "You can take it from me that three-quarters of what they say is not worth listening to!"

"Now you are being unkind, but actually I do think that you are right. I always find a man has much more to tell me about things I want to know about than a woman who, of course, ignores me as being totally irrelevant and concentrates her attentions on my Papa."

"I expect he enjoys it," Lord Springdale remarked.

"I am not certain that he does," Mellina answered. "He is always thinking of money and how he could make more. Although he adored my mother, he spent a great deal of his time away from her."

She spoke a little wistfully.

Then she added,

"But I am sure that if Mama was alive she would think I was doing the right thing now in running away with you."

She hesitated before she went on,

"Otherwise I could very easily find myself married to that terrible man who was, I know, only interested in the money Papa was giving me."

"How can you be so sure?" Lord Springdale asked.

Mellina did not answer him for a moment.

Then she said,

"I have read how the Greeks believe in the *Third Eye*. I think, although I don't want to use it, that everyone of us has a *Third Eye*, which is there if we need it."

She thought that he was listening, so she continued,

"One's *Third Eye* tells one the truth, the real truth, not what people want one to believe, but what one actually sees and feels for oneself."

"That is a subject I have not thought of before," he said. "I remember at school reading about the *Third Eye* and thinking it was an asset I would like to have myself, but I never really believed that I had one."

"Of course you have one," Mellina answered. "We all have one, but we are too lazy or too ignorant to realise how very special it is. If you look at a person with your *Third Eye*, then you know what they are really like."

She gave a little shiver before she went on,

"It was my *Third Eye* that told me the man, who I might be marrying at this very moment, is both greedy and evil."

"I can see," he replied, "that I have to polish up my *Third Eye*, which you say I have. We will soon see whether the people we might meet on this voyage are going to be significant in our lives or merely rubbish to be thrust out of sight rather than waste time on them."

Mellina gave a little jump of pleasure.

"You understand! You really do understand!" she cried. "When I have talked about this to other people, they have always pooh-poohed the idea and said that I should not waste my time fabricating silly ideas."

"I don't think you are doing that," Lord Springdale answered. "Equally you are giving me new ideas to think about, which up to now have, shall we say, not come my way."

"That is a compliment I really appreciate," Mellina replied. "But you know as well as I do that, if I talked about our *Third Eye* in a ballroom or discussed it with one of the young men had who asked me to dance, they would think that I was not in the slightest clever or unusual but merely idiotic!"

She smiled as she added,

"That is why, although I think about such matters, I very seldom mention them."

"But you are mentioning them to me, Mellina."

"Only because I know or rather my *Third Eye* is telling me, that you are much cleverer than you pretend to be. Although I suspected it before I came on board, now when I see these books and realise you have given them a cabin all to themselves, I know that you are very different from what I might have expected."

Lord Springdale laughed.

Then he said,

"I could say that I will have to brush up my brains to keep up with you. But I now suggest as the yacht is well underway and I am sure you will want to see the English Channel as we pass through it tomorrow, that we now go to bed. Can you manage to undo yourself? Or do you want any help?"

"I can manage perfectly, thank you," she replied. "But if not, I can hammer on your door and ask you to help me."

"As this is a new crew," he said, "I told them that we would unpack our own trunks and later the Captain will provide us with a man who is usually French, who will act as valet to me and a lady's maid to you."

Mellina laughed.

"I see that you think of every comfort, Ian. You are quite right and I would much rather take out the clothes I will want on board myself and leave the others until I need them."

She picked up another book as she spoke.

And then she walked out of the door and across the passage towards her cabin.

"I never thought anything would be so luxurious on a yacht," she said, "as to have a library next door and know that there are enough books there to keep me interested for at least a year."

"And are you really staying with me so long?" Lord Springdale asked with a smile.

Mellina grinned.

"How frightened you would be if I said 'yes'," she answered. "We must be absolutely frank with each other, Ian. If you are beginning to find me a bore, you must say so."

She paused before she went on,

"It will be quite easy for you to turn the yacht round and make it take me back to England at full speed."

"I am certain that that will not happen," he replied. "Not while you can talk to me about *Third Eyes* and all the other mysteries that I knew about but have forgotten."

"Well, I will remind you of them," she promised, "and thank you more than I can ever say for bringing me here in this beautiful yacht with such a fascinating library next door."

"What you should really be saying is that you have a handsome and exciting sailor next door!"

Mellina laughed.

"Do you really mean yourself?" she asked. "That is certainly new, I had not thought of you as a sailor before. Perhaps, as they are always at sea, sailors think differently and feel differently from the way that we do when we are walking about on dry land."

Lord Springdale put up his hands and gave a cry.

"Now you are stirring up my brain with a new idea just before I retire to bed. I will lie awake thinking over whether you are right or wrong. You must keep such ideas to yourself or bring them out at breakfast. That gives me a whole day to contemplate them, which I will undoubtedly do."

He was speaking in a mocking voice and Mellina laughed.

"Well, at least," she said, "you will not be bored with me until tomorrow morning. By that time we ought to be some way away from home."

Lord Springdale chuckled and said,

"Go to bed, Mellina, before you give me any more ideas. Perhaps I will feel strong enough tomorrow to argue with you."

"I do hope you will. It would be terribly dull if we agreed on every subject. But I agree on one thing and that is both of us need a good night's rest after all that has happened."

"I am thankful for small mercies," he retorted. "So goodnight, Mellina, and are you quite certain that you can manage to undo your dress or do you want my assistance?"

"I can manage, Ian, but thank you for thinking of it and thank you, thank you for bringing me here! It is so exciting and wonderful that I am still feeling that I must be dreaming."

There was a sincerity in the way she spoke that was very moving.

It passed through Lord Springdale's mind that he might kiss her goodnight.

Then he told himself that it might be a mistake.

He walked over to the door of his cabin and pushed it open.

"Goodnight, Mellina!" he called out. "Tomorrow we will make plans, but as it is getting late I think we both need our beauty sleep."

"I will not be worrying about what I look like," Mellina replied, "but what is inside these two marvellous books. Goodnight, Ian, and God Bless you! You are the kindest man in all the world."

"I only hope that your *Third Eye* is watching to see that you are not lying," he replied with a grin.

Then he walked into his own cabin and closed the door.

Mellina was laughing as she shut hers.

Then she looked longingly at the two books she had put down on the bed.

Because she felt that she must do what he wanted rather than what she desired, she started to undress.

*

Lord Springfield woke early as he always did even when he had been very late at some party or when he had walked home in the early hours after making love to some lovely woman, who had invariably begged him not to leave her.

He had learnt of old that it was a mistake to make the climax of the evening spread out too long.

He had therefore forced himself to leave despite the pleading of the women he had already spent several hours with.

After he had dressed himself in his white trousers and the comfortable jacket he wore when he was at sea, he went out on deck.

The sun was just climbing up the sky and the sea was smooth and silky.

It was a time when the world seemed to waken that he had always found particularly delightful.

He recalled how often in his life he had thought that a new day created a new beginning to everything.

He had often hoped that things that were wrong and unpleasant faded away with the darkness of the night.

He stood on deck gazing out to sea.

He realised that they were now some way down the English Channel and verging on the French coastline.

He stood at the rail and then moved towards the helm of the ship.

To his surprise, he found when he reached it that Mellina was there before him.

She turned as he appeared and smiled at him.

With the early sun on her face and her fair hair, he thought that she looked particularly enchanting.

"I did not expect to find you up and about so early," he greeted her.

"But how could I stay in bed with the sun glittering through the portholes?" she questioned. "I felt the waves were calling to me."

"Now you are becoming poetical," Lord Springdale teased. "I am just wondering what else I might discover about you before we come to the end of our voyage."

"One thing I love more than anything else is being at sea," Mellina said. "I find the waves fascinating and feel that every time they splash against the bow they are telling us something new and something exciting maybe about the countries in front of us or perhaps what lies at the bottom of the sea itself."

She spoke quietly.

There was a note of excitement in her voice which told him that she was absolutely honest in what she was saying and there was no pretence about it.

So many women he had associated with would say what they knew would attract him but were not in any way sincere.

"Tell me what you think lies at the bottom of the sea?" he ventured.

Mellina laughed.

"Mermaids of course and doubtless they will know far better than we do what the sea has suffered in the past centuries while the people on land were fighting and killing each other."

Lord Springdale was listening intently and she went on,

"At the same time frantically trying to make money rather than enjoy the magnificent gifts we have received from nature herself."

Lord Springdale flung up his hands.

"Now you are making me think far too early in the morning," he complained, "and when I just want to enjoy myself."

"Why should you not enjoy yourself when you are thinking?" Mellina asked seriously.

"Because it is almost painful to think out new ideas and new beliefs," he replied, "and admit that you had not thought of them before!"

Mellina laughed.

"We have so much to think about on this trip and I don't want to miss any of it, not even one drop of the sea or one cloud in the sky," she answered him.

"Now you are being greedy and that reminds me, although doubtless you enjoyed dinner as I did last night, I am feeling very hungry now, so, before you think up any more distractions, I suggest that we now go inside and ask for our breakfast."

"Tomorrow I will try to get up at dawn," Mellina said. "I missed the sun coming up in the sky and it was there before I was. Even so it was very thrilling and very beautiful and certainly something you should not miss."

"Very well, teacher!" Lord Springdale remarked. "But I still want my breakfast!"

"Then, of course, if your tummy speaks loudest, we must do what you want, Ian." Mellina answered.

She turned and ran soundlessly along the deck.

He had so often had women who arrived with high-heeled shoes, which made an awful clattering noise on the deck.

They were also dangerous if the ship was rolling in a high sea.

As he followed her into the Saloon, he realised that she was wearing a very pretty cotton dress.

Because it was too early for the sun to be warm, she wore it over a pale blue woollen jacket with bright buttons made of silver.

They sparkled in the sunshine and seemed to Lord Springdale to continue to sparkle in the Saloon.

As he had always appreciated women who dressed well and had been very sorry for those who had no taste, he recognised that Mellina was well dressed.

It was indeed something that her father could easily pay for.

The Saloon table had already been laid last night for breakfast.

The moment they appeared a Steward slipped away and came back carrying a tray with bacon and eggs on it and warm dishes.

There were rolls and *croissants* that had obviously just been taken from the kitchen oven and another Steward followed with pots of both tea and coffee.

"Do you want me to pour for you?" Mellina asked.

"Of course," Lord Springdale replied. "I expect women to wait on me at meals and it is their prerogative to arrange them for us men. On most occasions they reserve their authority to choose the menu for every meal."

"Is that what your previous guests did?" Mellina asked. "I am certain that the chef did not think it at all funny."

"You are so right. The chef, who was a Frenchman, was extremely annoyed when anyone interfered and asked for dishes which were essentially English and he did not think them at all appropriate for me."

"I can imagine the poor man must have been very upset. Tell me if you are a *gourmet* or do you, like most Englishmen, like big pieces of meat surrounded with lots of potatoes?"

"I enjoy good food especially when it is cooked by a Frenchman," Lord Springdale told her.

"That is a very good answer. But good food is very essential as it keeps us alive. Far too many people don't think of what they eat except as something tempting and pleasant."

"How do you think of food, Mellina?" he asked.

"I think food is important because if we don't eat we cannot think," she replied. "Therefore the food we eat must feed our bodies and make them strong and they must also stimulate our minds so that our brain is working to its fullest extent."

Lord Springdale stared at her.

"You are the most extraordinary young woman I have ever met," he said. "Do you think out all these ideas yourself or have you had a teacher?"

"I have always found that teachers think only on the subject they are proficient in," she replied. "What we have to think of is people. What is often forgotten is that every one of us is different. Every one of us requires food for our brain as for our body. In the majority of cases the food for the brain is either scanty or badly inscribed or often untrue and therefore dangerous."

He could not help being surprised at her reply.

And that she was speaking without being the least self-conscious.

"How can you possibly think of all this," he asked, "when you are so young? At your age you should just be thinking of enjoying yourself and, of course, flirting with all the men who admire you."

"What they admire," Mellina said after a moment's pause, "is Papa's money and, if I am being a bore when I talk about the matters that interest me, you must tell me not to bother you about them."

She stopped for breath before she continued,

"Then I will try to concentrate on horses, cricket and naturally yachts!"

"I like you saying what you are thinking," he said. "But it is not what I expect from a young girl. In fact to be honest I thought that they knew very little about the world and even less about human beings."

He smiled as he carried on,

"I just believed that they were primarily interested in their looks, what they are wearing and, of course, more important than anything else, how many compliments they receive."

Mellina laughed.

"How can you be so unkind?" she questioned him. "Of course we think of other things. But, as we are never encouraged to express them, they gradually disappear and are then forgotten."

"Then why are you different from the majority of girls, who I admit I find extremely boring and usually have nothing of any originality to say?"

"I think that is unfair," Mellina replied. "We are not encouraged as a rule to express what we feel or think. We are only asked silly questions like,

'Do you enjoy dancing?'

'Are you playing tennis this Season?'

Or worst of all, 'may I kiss you?'"

Lord Springdale threw back his head and laughed.

"And so how many times have you said, 'yes'?" he asked.

"I have never been kissed and I do *not* intend to be until I find what we have set out to find," she answered. "That is true love, the love that we both want, but we are far too shy to talk about."

"Now it is my turn to say I think that is unkind," he retorted. "We have discussed it. We have said that it is our El Dorado and that we are determined to find it."

"And that is exactly why you are different from the other men I have met," Mellina said. "At the same time it is somewhat difficult to put into words what it means to us. Therefore I doubt if we will talk about it very much even if we think about it."

"You are quite right," Lord Springdale agreed, "it is hard to put into words, especially at breakfast. But, as you say, it is what we are both trying to find. Therefore we must be entirely frank with each other in what we see, hear or discover."

He paused before he continued and there was now a serious note in his voice,

"It would be very sad to miss it altogether if we were too shy to speak about it."

"We will certainly not do that," Mellina answered. "But I don't want to bore you with listening to what I feel or what I think when I should be listening to all that you have to tell me."

"Of course we must be frank with each other," he agreed. "But you must be aware that you are not talking to me as an ordinary young woman of the *Beau Monde* would nor do you in any way resemble any of those rather boring *debutantes*, who have been continually pressed on me by their ambitious mothers ever since I left school and long before I ended up at Oxford University."

Mellina laughed.

"Of course every mother tries her best to find the ideal husband for her daughter and it is only right that she should do so. The unfortunate aspect is that they don't for a moment consider that their daughters are able to think for themselves."

"Is that what happens?" Lord Springdale asked.

"Of course it is," Mellina replied. "The mothers of *debutantes* want what they consider to be the best for their daughters so they start at the top of the Social tree with a Duke and go slowly and reluctantly down to a mere Knight at the very bottom!"

He chuckled.

And then Mellina added,

"Eventually it can be a choice between a Colonel in the Army or a Midshipman in the Navy. After that the story has no history!"

He was laughing again as Mellina finished speaking and started to pour out her coffee.

CHAPTER FOUR

The Bay of Biscay was no rougher than it usually was.

At the same time surging waves broke over the bow of the yacht one after the other.

It was very difficult to walk on deck unless one was particularly careful.

At any moment a big wave, for no obvious reason, would break over the sides.

If one was not quick enough in avoiding them, one was soaked to the skin.

Mellina was very sensible, when she went outside, to wear a mackintosh over her dress.

She appeared to glory in the fact that, as the yacht progressed Southwards, the huge waves seemed to break more violently against its sides.

To Lord Springdale's astonishment Mellina was not seasick.

At dinner when everything that could be held down on the table was fixed, he asked her,

"How can it be possible that unlike other women you are not seasick?"

"I don't know," Mellina replied. "But I believe that there must be some very good reason, perhaps it is what I eat. But we ought to discover what it is and sell it for large sums of money to everyone who is going to sea."

"It's certainly a good idea," Lord Springdale said. "But I would suspect that people have been trying since the beginning of time to avoid the dreaded seasickness. So it must be something hardy in your blood."

"Perhaps that's true," Mellina reflected.

He found that, when they took their meals together, she always had something unusual and interesting to say.

They argued on a great number of subjects, but he had to admit that she was extremely clever in producing something he had never heard of before to support her arguments.

*

When they left the Bay of Biscay behind them, they arrived at Gibraltar.

They moved into the magnificent Port fairly early in the morning.

The sun was now shining brightly and Mellina said excitedly to Lord Springdale,

"Please, I do want to go ashore. I want to see the monkeys I have heard so much about. And the shops that I am told are all filled with wonderful things from different countries especially China."

"Why from China particularly?" he asked.

"Because I love the embroidery they do better than any other country," Mellina explained. "They also have original ideas in China on glass."

He thought it strange that a young girl should be so interested in what other countries produced.

Equally she was absolutely right about Gibraltar as he had been there a number of times in the past.

He had always been very impressed with the shawls that came from China and the many other items that were on sale from almost every country in the world.

"Well, come along," he said when their breakfast was finished, "let's get our shopping over with. Then I can take you up to where you will have a closer view of the monkeys than on the lower ground."

"That will be wonderful!" Mellina exclaimed.

They then walked along the quayside to where they could see the shops at the end of a long wide road.

Already there were a number of customers staring at the shop windows.

"I tell you what I will give you," Lord Springdale said, "and that is a Chinese shawl and then when we reach our next Port of call you can buy me a present."

"I would certainly like to do that, Ian. Actually I should be giving you a present at every Port we stop at because that will be one way of paying for my passage."

"You need not worry about that," he said. "You only occupy one cabin and you drink far less than most of my guests manage to consume especially when we are in the Bay of Biscay!"

Mellina grinned.

"I can imagine them drinking and thinking it would be an anti-seasickness medicine."

"I believe champagne and port can be that if you drink enough of them," he replied. "But I noticed that you kept to lemonade."

"The lemonade that your chef makes is delicious," Mellina said. "I think that champagne should be kept for weddings, funerals and birthdays. I was always given a tiny glass with a teaspoonful in it to drink Papa's and Mama's health on their birthdays. And to tell the truth, personally, I prefer lemonade."

"It is certainly a far cheaper way of celebrating our journey," Lord Springdale replied. "But now let's go and explore the shops."

Mellina was absolutely thrilled with the beautiful embroidered shawl he gave her.

She thought that no one but the Chinese could have made it more original.

The only thing that worried her was when she learnt that small children were made to work in China. They were responsible for much of the exquisite embroidery that she could see hanging outside the shops, which made Gibraltar such a place of colour and originality.

Lord Springdale was paying for the shawl Mellina had finally chosen and the shopkeeper was wrapping it in a piece of tissue paper when a voice rang out,

"Ian, darling, is it really you?"

Mellina then turned to see a very attractive smartly dressed woman.

She boasted long sweeping dark eyelashes over her eyes, which had a touch of green in them.

"Florentina!" he exclaimed. "Can it be you?"

"It is, and I am so thrilled, darling Ian, to see you again. Why have you not been to Paris lately? I have been hoping and hoping that you would turn up unexpectedly."

"I have been very busy in London with my horses," Lord Springdale answered.

"Horses! Horses!" the woman then echoed. "They always mean far more to you than anyone else and every woman you have ever known is jealous – not of another woman – but of your latest and swiftest horse!"

He laughed.

Putting her hand on his chest, she then said,

"Tell me you have missed me. Tell me you have been longing to see me again. Oh, darling, darling, it has been so dull without you!"

There was a note in her voice that made Mellina feel that she was almost in tears at the thrill of seeing him again.

Then, because she felt it might be embarrassing for him to explain why he was with her, she slipped away.

Moving through the other people on the street, she went towards the shops.

She then started to run very quickly along the quay and back to where the yacht was anchored.

It was only when she was in her cabin and had put her present down on the bed did she wonder if the beautiful lady, and she was indeed extremely beautiful, would give him the love he was searching for.

Sitting down at the dressing table she looked in the mirror and saw the lovely face of the woman she had left talking to Lord Springdale.

'Perhaps this is the one he is seeking,' she thought to herself. 'And, if she is, then maybe we will go back to England. Although I have run away, I will have to return to Papa and that awful man who wants to marry me will be waiting for me.'

She trembled at the mere idea of it.

Then she felt as if a dark cloud was falling over her because this might be the end of the voyage.

'I have never been so happy,' she told herself. 'I have never enjoyed anything so much and, if it comes to an end so soon, I suppose I should not grumble."

She gave a deep sigh.

Then to her surprise she heard Lord Springdale call her name.

A moment later he knocked and then opened her cabin door.

"Oh, here you are!" he exclaimed. "I wondered where you had gone, but thought that you would have the common sense to come back to the yacht."

Mellina hesitated for a moment.

Then she said rather incoherently,

"I thought perhaps – it would be difficult to explain who I was and – why I was with you."

"In other words you were being tactful," he replied. "It was very sensible of you. But I was worried in case you had got lost in the crowd or tried to climb up to see the monkeys by yourself."

"I came – here," Mellina said stumbling a little over her words, "in case – I lost your beautiful present."

"You must wear it tonight at dinner," he suggested. "As we are both back and the Captain is anxious to be on his way, we might as well tell him to start the engines and set sail."

Mellina's eyes lit up.

"You have not asked your lady friend to come with us?" she enquired.

"No, of course not," he replied quickly. "Luckily she did not see you or ask any questions. She is a terrible gossip and, if she had been aware I had a lady on board with me, which naturally she suspected, the whole of Paris would be talking about it in the next day or so."

Mellina felt her spirits rise and she was glad that she had slipped away from an awkward situation.

"Now I am just going to speak to the Captain and tell him to go ahead," he said. "I think that we might stop at Marseilles. There is a very good restaurant I remember where they have delicious fish cooked as only the French can cook fish and it will only that morning have come in from the sea."

"That sounds superb," Mellina answered excitedly, "and I would love to go there."

"I think you would enjoy it," he replied. "So I will go and tell the Captain to sail off for Marseilles."

As Lord Springdale left the cabin, Mellina gave a sigh of contentment.

She thought that she had been very stupid to be frightened of the beautiful lady, who had been so effusive to his Lordship.

'I thought for a moment,' she told herself, 'that our adventure had come to an end. But thank You, thank You God, for letting it continue and everything is very thrilling. I have never felt as happy as I am at this moment.'

As she finished the prayer in her mind, she went to the porthole to watch the open sea.

Only when they were well away from Gibraltar did she go up on deck.

The sun was shining brightly and the Mediterranean was exactly the magic blue that it was always reported to be.

She went to the bow to watch the sea breaking on the sides of the yacht as they moved through it.

She thought, as she had already, that she had never felt so blissfully happy.

She knew that Lord Springdale was on the bridge with the Captain and that she was the only passenger on board.

She could not help thinking that if they had been joined by the effusive lady, who had been so pleased to see him, she would have been ignored or forgotten.

She would also have felt very *de trop* when she was talking in such a loving way to him.

After being in the Bay of Biscay, the Mediterranean was smooth and serene.

Mellina felt almost as if they were dancing on the sea, rather than battling their way through it.

When they arrived at Marseilles, it was midday.

Lord Springdale was determined to take her to the place where he remembered they had served such delicious dishes straight from the sea.

The restaurant itself was built almost on the sand above the beach.

Mellina commented that they might, as they looked out of the windows, still be at sea.

Lord Springdale was received with all the delight the French usually reserve for their guests when they return after a long absence.

They were escorted immediately to the best table, which was in the window.

There was the usual lengthy talk of what fish had come in that morning from the local small fishing boats.

The chef was told that he was to produce his best and most acclaimed dish for the very distinguished diners.

A special champagne was brought to the table for Lord Springdale's approval.

There was the usual wait while the fish, which was shown to them in a bucket of water, was transformed into a delicious dish.

While they were waiting, Mellina persuaded Lord Springdale to tell her of his previous visits to Marseilles.

There had been quite a number of them and he was in the middle of saying how amusing it had been on one occasion when the whole City was celebrating some feast day when their *patron* came to the table to say,

"As you are here, *monsieur*, you must go to the ball which is being given tonight at *Le Crayon*."

Lord Springdale raised his eyebrows.

"I don't remember a place of that name," he said.

"It has just opened," the *patron* told him. "It is a new hotel with a very large dance floor. Tonight is to be a very special occasion because they have brought a big band from Paris to play for the dancers. There is to be a cotillion at the end when everyone will receive marvellous prizes."

"Oh, I would love to go to that!" Mellina piped up without thinking.

Then she glanced quickly at Lord Springdale as if she thought that she was now asking for something that he might disapprove of.

Instead, he said to the *patron*,

"It sounds entertaining. Please book me a special table and I suppose it starts very late."

"*Non, non, monsieur*. You go at nine o'clock. Not for dinner but for supper which I am informed will be just *supreme*."

The *patron* kissed his fingers as he mouthed the last word.

Lord Springdale laughed.

"Then we must only eat a small amount before we go there. But it certainly sounds most entertaining."

"It is very amusing, *monsieur*," the *patron* insisted, "and something that you should not miss on your visit to our beautiful City."

He then hurried away to the kitchen to see if their fish was cooked.

"So do you really want to go out tonight?" Mellina asked. "I will be disappointed if you refuse. At the same time we have been sensible enough to go to bed early every night so far."

"I think that there should be an exception to every rule," Lord Springdale replied.

He smiled at Mellina before he added,

"I do want you to enjoy yourself ashore as well as aboard. In fact we would be very stupid to miss seeing the

French idea of a special occasion and Marseilles is in many ways a law unto itself."

"What you mean," Mellina said, "is that it does not imitate the ways of Paris."

"That is exactly right," he replied. "Paris has been the ultimate word for gaiety and amusement for the whole of Europe. If you ask me, Marseilles is now ready to do combat with Paris."

Mellina grinned.

"You make them sound like two people fighting to win a prize."

"That is just what they are," Lord Springdale said. "As we are in Marseilles, we might as well back them and hope that they will be successful in the admiration they are fighting to obtain internationally."

Their luncheon, as predicted, was delicious. Every course was sublime, but the *pièce de resistance* of the fresh fish literally melted in the mouth.

When it was over, Lord Springdale suggested that they should walk back to the yacht.

"It's now getting very hot," he said, "and, as you are going to be late tonight, I don't want you falling asleep before we have sung the *Marseillaise* at the end of the evening and congratulated the *patron* of the hotel, who I should imagine will be our host."

"I am so glad I brought my best evening dress with me," Mellina said. "Even then I cannot expect to be as smart as the French."

"I think that actually you will compete very well," Lord Springdale said reassuringly.

She hoped that he meant it.

But, when she was dressing later, she wondered if he would regret having to take her to the party and would rather have been with someone sophisticated like the lady they had encountered at Gibraltar.

She was certainly very beautiful and self-assured.

'If he is trying to find someone more enchanting than her,' she thought to herself as she dressed, 'he might well be disappointed.'

She was gazing in the mirror at her reflection at the time and thought that in contrast to the French women she would look rather dull.

She did not have that particular *chic* that was so much a part of the French.

"I am English and I look English," she said firmly to the mirror.

She felt very apologetic when she went up to the Saloon where Lord Springdale was waiting for her.

He had said that they would be expected to eat an enormous amount of food as soon as they arrived at the party.

Although they had enjoyed delicious cakes for tea, they had not had anything to eat later.

As she entered the Saloon, Lord Springdale looked at her approvingly and said,

"That is a very pretty dress. In fact it is one of the prettiest I have seen for some time. I am certain that our French friends will really appreciate it."

Mellina was delighted.

The dress she wore was one that had cost a great deal of money and she had been told when she purchased it in Bond Street that it came from Paris.

But, as they said that about everything which was at all outstanding, she was very suspicious that after all it was English from top to bottom, actually because it was a very pretty soft pink embroidered with diamanté round the neck and sleeves.

It made Mellina glitter like the fairy on a Christmas tree.

The full skirt falling from her tiny waist made her appear very different from the usual English girl abroad.

And there were flowers sparkling in her hair.

Lord Springdale was thinking to himself that every man he knew would say that as usual he had captured the best of the bunch.

"Come on," he said, "we are off to enjoy ourselves and I have told the Captain to move the yacht out of Port early tomorrow morning, but not to wake us while he is doing so."

"It is very exciting for me to be going to this party." Mellina replied "especially a French one. I found all the parties I attended in London were much of a muchness, but this will be something very new that I have never done before."

"I thought that was the real point of this evening," he answered. "We both want to try different things and it would be ridiculous at your age to be a fuddy-duddy and never to try anything new."

Mellina threw up her hands.

"I will try anything new you wish me to and I am sure it will be a scintillating experience," she replied.

When they arrived at the hotel, they found that the room where the party was to take place was down on the lower floor.

The far end of the building opened straight onto the beach.

It was decorated with streamers of every size and colour and the band was already playing a bright tune that made Mellina feel that she wanted to dance right away.

There were tables all round the room most of which were already occupied.

The table that had been booked for them was just to the side of the window opening onto the beach.

Lord Springdale thought they would be grateful for the fresh air by the time the room was completely full and everyone was dancing.

The supper, which came at once, was delicious.

The band played soft tunes while the room filled up with a crowd of revellers and this made it seem even more exciting than Mellina had expected.

It was impossible to talk above the voices, the band and the movement of those who had already taken to the dance floor.

She could only look round her, watch and eat.

The food and all the wines were excellent and very French.

She felt that, although the women were exceedingly smart, the men present could in no way compete with Lord Springdale.

Because he was so tall and so handsome, he seemed almost like a Fairy Prince amongst them.

It was when they had finished the last course of their supper that Lord Springdale proposed,

"Now we must dance. I feel that quite a number of people will want to admire your dress as we move round the floor.

He did not wait for her to reply, but put his arm round her.

She found that he was an even better dancer than she had expected him to be.

The music was getting louder and, Lord Springdale thought, quicker, as the men began to swing their women relentlessly round the room.

It was difficult to move through the crowd which had now increased considerably.

He was aware that large though the dance hall was, a number of people had seats in the corridor outside.

There were even people coming from upstairs, who could not find a table as they were all taken.

As the music seemed to get louder and even noisier than it was already, Lord Springdale was about to suggest that they sit down as they had been dancing for some time, when unexpectedly the conductor went to the centre of the stage where the band was playing.

In French he called out,

"All change partners! All change partners!"

Even as he finished shouting the words, the band burst into an even noisier and faster dance than they had played before.

Before either of them realised what was happening, they found themselves dancing with a different partner.

Mellina's man was the one that she had realised had been watching her ever since she had been dancing on the floor with Lord Springdale.

His table was not far from theirs and she was aware that he had been gazing at her a great deal while they were eating their supper.

Now, as he was holding her rather too tightly as they danced around briskly, her *Third Eye* told her that he was not a particularly pleasant man.

Nor did she think that he was very well-bred, but he was obviously delighted at being her partner.

As they moved with difficulty around the crowded floor, Mellina decided that there was definitely something rather disagreeable about him.

She hoped that their dance together would not last for very long.

It seemed as though it was a part of the evening's entertainment that the band should grow noisier and noisier to force the dancers to move even quicker than they were already.

It was then that her partner began to talk.

He told her in French that he thought she was the most beautiful woman he had ever seen.

And that having found her he was determined not to lose her.

Lord Springdale had found himself dancing with a rather pretty but not so young woman.

She was, however, reasonably attractive in a subtle French manner.

He guessed that she was an employee of the hotel before she told him in no uncertain terms what she wanted.

He shook his head.

"I am sorry," he said. "But I am here tonight with someone who is staying with me and I am afraid I cannot leave her."

"I am sure that she will find someone as amusing as you must be," the woman answered him. "I will be very disappointed, *mon brave*, if you don't let me show you how happy I can make you."

"I am sorry, but it is impossible," Lord Springdale asserted.

Then, as the music continued, he told her,

"I think I must now go to my table to see what has happened to the *mademoiselle* I brought here with me."

The woman he was dancing with was however very persistent that he should not leave her.

She clung to him in a way that made it difficult for him to free himself from her grasp.

The music did not stop.

But then a number of partners seemed to disappear off the floor and back into the hotel.

Lord Springdale realised, as he thought he should have realised earlier, that this was not a place he should have brought Mellina to.

He was now determined to take her away before she found out what was happening.

Then to his consternation he could not find her.

He looked round the room peering in between the dancing couples, but there was no sign of her.

He wondered if maybe she had been foolish enough to listen to her partner's pleading that might easily have been exactly the same as he had received from his.

But Mellina would not be experienced enough to know how refuse him firmly.

'I have to find her,' he told himself.

Almost abruptly he shook himself free from the girl he was dancing with.

"You must excuse me," he said in French, "but I have a duty to look after the lady who is very young who accompanied me here."

The woman he was dancing with protested loudly as he went back to the table.

His bill was waiting for him and he paid it quickly, but still there was no sign of Mellina.

He then walked back into the huge ballroom and wondered how he could find her.

Because he was so worried, he went into the front of the hotel and asked two of the staff at the door if they had seen the young lady he had arrived with since they had been downstairs.

The two men said that they had not seen her.

Another man, who was standing outside the door to open the carriage doors of late arrivals, told him that there was a young lady in the carriage they had arrived in.

For a moment Lord Springdale just stared at him.

As the man pointed out the carriage that had picked them up, which he had told to wait for his return, he ran towards it.

It was parked a little way from the front door.

As there were a number of other carriages near to it, which looked very much the same, he was half-afraid that he would go to the wrong one.

Then, as he reached it and pulled open the door, he saw with a sense of utter relief that she was sitting alone on the back seat.

The driver, who had been half-asleep, woke up as he opened the door.

As he peered down, Lord Springdale ordered him,

"Take us back to the Port *toute suite*!"

Then he climbed into the carriage.

As he closed the door and sat down beside Mellina, he said,

"I lost you and I just could not imagine what had happened to you."

"I was frightened," Mellina whispered, "so – I ran away from the man I had to dance with – and managed to slip out here and find the carriage we came in."

"That was very clever of you," he replied. "I am so sorry if you were upset by your partner."

"He was horrid. He suggested that I should go – up to the room where he was staying."

She gave a shiver as she spoke and had difficulty in telling him what had happened to her.

As if he knew only too well what the Frenchman must have said and expected, Lord Springdale said quickly,

"Forget it! It was a mistake for us to go there, but I did not realise what sort of place it was until we were forced into dancing with strangers."

Mellina put her hand into his.

"It was horrid," she said, "I kept feeling that he was like the man Papa – wants me to marry. It was difficult to get – away from him."

"But you managed it," he said, "and please don't let it spoil your visit to France. Forget it and just remember what a good meal we had."

He felt her fingers tighten on his as she said,

"I knew I would be safe if I found you, but I could not see you – in such a huge crowd."

"And I could not see you, Mellina. Now just forget what happened. The evening has now finished and we are going back to the yacht where we are safe from Frenchmen and Frenchwomen. In fact tomorrow we are going right across the Mediterranean to North Africa."

He heard Mellina give a deep sigh and then felt her relax.

"I was – so frightened, Ian," she whispered.

"But you were quite astute enough to escape," Lord Springdale replied, "from what was unpleasant. Now that we are together again, it is just one adventure that has gone wrong."

Mellina gave a little laugh.

"Of course it is and it is so silly – of me to be upset. But I did not know there would be men – like that, who would appear from nowhere when I least expected it."

The horses were now moving rapidly down the hill towards the Port.

Lord Springdale lent back on the comfortable seat of the carriage.

"I think," he said quietly, "we both have to expect the unusual to happen because we are doing the unexpected ourselves in running away from London and seeking what few people are privileged enough to even attempt."

He looked thoughtful before he added,

"If we are seeking adventure, as we are, we must not complain too much if what we find is not exactly as we expected."

Mellina gave another little sigh.

Then she put her head against his shoulder.

"You are quite right," she said. "It was very stupid of me to be so frightened. But men like that I find very intimidating."

"Of course they are," he agreed. "Another time we will not allow ourselves to be separated."

There was silence and they drove on for some way before Lord Springdale suggested,

"We are nearly back at the yacht and, when you go to bed, just think what a delicious supper we had and the band was very good until it went mad."

"That is one way of looking at it, Ian. I certainly did enjoy the supper tonight as I so enjoyed the luncheon we had today."

"Then do forget everything else. Remember that all men are not like him, just as all women are, unfortunately, not like you."

Mellina laughed again.

"How bored you would become if they were!" she exclaimed.

Lord Springdale realised, as her hand slipped from his, that she was no longer afraid.

He thought that they had in fact been very fortunate in escaping so lightly from what might easily have turned nasty.

'I was a fool,' he thought, 'not to realise that was the sort of place it turned out to be. It is a mistake I will not make in the future.'

CHAPTER FIVE

The Captain had received his orders and they left the Port of Marseilles very early the next morning.

The sun was shining brilliantly and Mellina was so enchanted at the idea of visiting Tunis.

She knew from reading the English newspapers that the French had seized Tunisia the previous year and were now well established and firmly in control of the country.

The majority of the people there spoke French, so they would have little difficulty in communicating with the locals.

But Lord Springdale did not say too much about it being French after Mellina's experience in Marseilles.

They arrived some hours later at La Goulette, the Port in the Bay of Tunis, and at once found an excellent place where they could anchor the yacht.

As they were both tired after the previous night and there was no particular reason to hurry, they had breakfast late.

It was nearly ten o'clock when one of the Stewards came to say that there was a gentleman from the Embassy who wished to see them.

Lord Springdale looked surprised and the Steward handed him a card.

It was an embossed visiting card and had *'British Embassy'* written clearly at the top of it.

Lord Springdale read it and saw that their caller was the Honourable David Bentley.

He handed the card to Mellina, who looked at it and asked,

"I suppose we have to see him."

"It would be very impolite not to," Lord Springdale replied, "but let's go out on deck and sit in the sunshine."

He turned to the Steward and said,

"It's too early for a drink, but maybe we should ask our visitor if he would like a cup of coffee."

"I will see to it, sir," the Steward promised.

They walked out on deck and found a rather good-looking young man, very correctly dressed, who held out his hand saying,

"I have been told that you had arrived last night in a magnificent yacht and I thought it only polite to ask you, as you are from England, if there is anything that we at the Embassy can do for you, sir."

He paused for a moment before he added,

"The Ambassador, I regret to tell you, is in Cairo at the moment on an official mission and I am in charge and I will do anything I can to help you, if you so wish."

"It is extremely kind of you," Lord Springdale said. "I expect you know that my name is Ian Blakeley and this is my sister, Mellina, who is accompanying me on a trip to see what are to her new places of interest."

The young man shook hands with Mellina.

They then moved across the deck to sit down in a shady place where comfortable chairs had been arranged round a table.

"I thought perhaps it was a bit too early to offer you a drink," Lord Springdale said, "but I feel sure that you would like a cup of coffee."

"As I had breakfast early, I would be very grateful," David Bentley said. "In fact I am finding the task of being acting Ambassador rather difficult as too people think that the British Embassy is where they can bring every possible complaint. And, believe it or not, I have to listen to half-a-dozen every day."

Lord Springdale laughed.

"We are very sorry for you, but we are not able to help you, although I am sure that you could help us."

"What can I do for you, sir?" David Bentley asked him.

"Well we are very anxious, both of us, to visit the Colosseum at El Djem," Lord Springdale replied. "What we want to know is if we can hire two horses to take us to it as we have no desire to walk for miles."

David Bentley laughed.

"You will not have to do that. There are excellent horses you can hire at the small fishing village of Mahdia, which is not far from the Colosseum and you can anchor the yacht there without any difficulty."

"That is what I wanted to hear," Lord Springdale smiled, "and I am very grateful to you for the information."

The Steward then arrived with a steaming pot of hot coffee.

It was poured out on a small table placed in front of them.

"Before you leave here," David Bentley said, "I am sure that Miss Blakeley would like to pay a visit to the City of Tunis."

"Of course I would," Mellina answered excitedly, "and do tell me about your Embassy. Is it new and smart?"

"We think it is," he replied. "And, if you would like to see it, would you be able to come to dinner tonight? And

I can definitely promise you an excellent dinner as naturally our chef is French."

Mellina laughed.

"You could not do better and we have been saying so ever since we left Gibraltar."

"Thank you very much, we will be very delighted to dine with you," Lord Springdale confirmed. "What time would you like us to be there?"

"Shall we say around seven-thirty?" David Bentley suggested. "I don't suppose that you would like the French habit of not dining until late?"

"Certainly not," Lord Springdale said. "Although we are interested in seeing Tunisia, we are determined to keep the Union Jack flying!"

They chuckled and then David Bentley remarked,

"The French have their good points especially when it comes to food. But they can be very tiresome in other ways as I have found ever since I came here."

"Have you been here long?" Lord Springdale asked him.

"Nearly a year," he replied. "I am hoping to go to a more exciting country when it is time for me to move on."

"And what would you call an exciting country?" Mellina asked.

"Well, if I am to be honest, I would really want to be posted to the East. I suppose that Constantinople would be very interesting, but most of all I would like to be sent to India."

He gave a sigh before he added,

"But I am afraid that I will have to wait for many years before I achieve that goal."

Lord Springdale smiled.

"Then you must do something dramatic," he said. "I have always found that, when someone is being talked about and has been brave or somehow caught the attention of the 'powers-that-be', they are always sent off to the best places in the future."

"That is certainly true," David Bentley agreed, "but I cannot think of anything I can do at the moment, except, of course, make sure that you enjoy your visit to Tunis and help in every way I can."

He was gazing at Mellina as he spoke.

Then Lord Springdale was thinking to himself that she had made a conquest and therefore promised that they would be at the Embassy at seven-thirty on the dot.

David Bentley said that he would send a carriage for them.

"I look forward to seeing your Embassy," Mellina said. "You must tell us what else we must see while we are in Tunis."

"I would suppose that the most unusual attraction for visitors," he said, "is that each street represents a single trade."

"What do you mean?" Mellina asked.

"The *Souk des Femmes* began catering for women coming on pilgrimage to the tomb of Sidi Mahrez," David Bentley explained. "There is the *Souk des Orfevres*, which is the home of gold and silversmiths, the *Souk de la Laine* for wool and the *Souk El Leffa* specialises in carpets and blankets, while the *Souk El Attarin* deals in perfumes."

"What a wonderful idea!" Mellina exclaimed. "I must go and see them and you must tell me where I can buy the best souvenirs to take back home with me."

"I would very much like to do that," David Bentley smiled.

Lord Springdale thought again with amusement that Mellina had certainly found an unexpected admirer.

It was with some difficulty that David Bentley drew himself away.

He said that there was a great deal of work waiting for him at the Embassy.

"I will be counting the hours until seven-thirty," he added, "when I can see you both again."

He said 'both', but again his eyes were on Mellina.

When he finally said goodbye and left them, Lord Springdale said to her,

"He is a rather nice young man and he is obviously very smitten with you."

"I doubt it," she replied. "He was just being polite as Embassies are always told to be. They have to make themselves agreeable to visitors who I am told invariably have lost their passports or run out of money."

Lord Springdale laughed.

"Well, I think that we should now go and do some shopping," he said. "I will tell one of the men to find us a carriage and we will drive to the town unless, of course, you can think of anything special you would like to do."

"I think we should drive to the town first," Mellina replied. "I am sure now the French have moved in that they have made it as much like Paris as it is possible for them to do."

Lord Springdale laughed again.

"The French always get back finally to the *Place Vendôme* and I think that if they had the choice they would have a small copy of it made to put on their tombs. To the French everything must be French just as in England we believe that no one could possibly be better than us."

He was speaking lightly, but Mellina said seriously,

"I think you are right, Ian. I think also that people should always believe that their own country is better than anyone else's."

She paused before she added,

"Otherwise they would always be changing where they lived and we would lose our individuality to everyone else."

It was the sort of remark that Mellina was often making.

It made Lord Springdale think again that she really was different from any woman he had ever met.

She had obviously read a great deal about the other countries in Europe.

They had had a spirited conversation the previous day as to which country had the most to give the world.

When the carriage arrived, they then went on shore to find that it was a very smart conveyance.

It had two seats behind the driver, who was slightly raised as in England, but their seats had no doors at the side and you could step straight into them from the ground.

Lord Springdale told the driver in French that they wanted to see the town and would he drive slowly through the most fashionable streets.

They set off and the two horses drawing them were rather frisky.

There was little doubt that the driver encouraged rather than prevented them from speeding.

As they then cantered round a corner at what Lord Springdale thought was rather a fast rate, there was a small boy playing in a puddle at the side of the road.

The carriage wheels, driving fast through the water, splashed him so that he fell backwards aghast.

They undoubtedly smashed whatever it was that he was playing with.

Their coachman would have driven on, but Lord Springdale ordered him to stop.

Before he could prevent her, Mellina sprang out of the carriage and ran down the side of the road to where the boy had been playing.

He had not been injured, but was crying because he was feeling frightened and because the carriage wheels had smashed what Mellina saw was a toy boat that he had been playing with in the puddle.

By the time Lord Springdale joined her, she had the boy in her arms and was comforting him.

"Don't cry, *mon petit*," she was saying in French. "You are not hurt and are only a little wet. The horses are very sorry they splashed you."

The boy, however, went on crying on her shoulder.

She held him close and continued to talk to him.

She made, Lord Springdale thought, a very pretty picture as she sat down on the pavement regardless of her dress and held the shaking boy in her arms.

As he joined them, she looked up to say,

"We smashed his boat and he is very sad because it was something he could sail all by himself. We must go and buy him another one, Ian."

"Yes, of course we must," he agreed.

He looked at the broken boat, which was floating on the puddle and remarked,

"I don't think that there is any point in saving this wreck."

"Not if we buy him another one," Mellina replied. "But it is rather dangerous for him to be playing in the road."

"I don't suppose they have much traffic in this part of the town," Lord Springdale answered. "It was bad luck that our driver was travelling so fast and took the corner unnecessarily sharply."

"I agree with you," Mellina said. "But it is a mistake to tell him so. Tell him we now want to go to the best toy shop in the town."

Still carrying the boy in her arms, she walked to the carriage, which was a little further up the road, and Lord Springdale followed her.

When she climbed into the carriage, she still held the boy on her knee.

But he had stopped crying and was excited at being in a horse-drawn carriage.

Lord Springdale then sat down beside them.

He was thinking that Mellina was the only woman of his acquaintance who would not have been in the least worried about the mud on her dress.

Or that it was wet as the small boy had been so splashed.

She was still talking to him in a soft cooing voice.

She was telling him about the yacht they had come in and how when he grew up perhaps he would be a sailor.

She spoke slowly and very gently to him.

Lord Springdale felt that there were few women he had known who would have taken so much trouble over a small child, who was not really hurt, only frightened.

Their driver found the toy shop.

It was not surprising that it was in the street which catered for women's clothes and anything of interest to the female.

There was a profusion of different toys for all ages.

But the boy whose name Mellina had discovered was Pierre was quickly fascinated by quite a large toy ship that was prominently displayed in the shop window.

Lord Springdale asked for the price of it and found that, although it was roughly made and gaudily painted, it was quite expensive.

In fact, he thought, too expensive for the average traveller to Tunis.

The woman in charge of the shop displayed a great number of other toys for them.

But the small boy was most insistent that the one he really wanted was the ship.

"*I* will buy it for him," Mellina said when Lord Springdale put his hand into his pocket.

"No, of course not," he replied. "It was my carriage that did the damage and it is obvious that the ship is the one toy that Pierre has set his heart on."

"I have brought a lot of money with me in case I had to go home unexpectedly," Mellina told him.

Lord Springdale smiled.

"Were you thinking that it would be in disgrace," he asked, "or because you were bored with my company?"

"I was merely afraid I might bore you," Mellina replied. "It would have been very presumptive if, after you were kind enough to take me away, that I had to ask you for every penny that I spent or my ticket home if you were fed up with my company."

Lord Springdale chuckled.

"You are quite safe so far," he said. "So I think you should keep your money in case of an emergency."

"Are you warning me that you might send me home before you find what you are seeking?" Mellina asked.

The shopkeeper was busily packing up the toy ship and the small boy was watching as if he could not believe that it was really going to belong to him.

The shop was empty, so there was no one to listen to their conversation.

Then Lord Springdale said,

"You may not need your money, but I am enjoying every moment of our adventure together and I think, with one exception only, that you are too."

"Of course I am," Mellina enthused. "And I have already forgotten how frightened I was in Marseilles and I cannot believe that there are nasty men waiting to terrify me here in Tunis."

"No, of course not," he agreed. "I will make quite certain that wherever we go, you are not intimidated in the same way as you and Pierre have been."

Mellina's eyes twinkled.

"Now I feel safe," she replied. "Having run away from danger twice, I am hoping that there will not be a third time."

Lord Springdale was smiling at her as Pierre gave a whoop of excitement because the toy ship was now nicely wrapped up and the shopkeeper had handed it to him.

"Now we had better take him home," Mellina said. "Otherwise I am sure that his mother will be frantic if she finds he is missing. Actually we should have let her know that we were taking him to the shop."

"I suppose we should have done," he agreed. "At the same time she should not allow her son to play in a puddle in the road when there is traffic passing by."

"Well, you tell her that when we see her," Mellina remarked. "I am just very grateful that the horses did not touch him or the wheels pass over him."

"Don't think about it," he urged her. "It will only worry you. I think that at the moment he is the happiest boy we would find anywhere in the whole of Tunis!"

There was no doubt that Pierre was thrilled with his present.

When they climbed back into the carriage, he held his package tightly in his arms as if he was afraid someone would take it away from him.

Mellina had him close to her and talked to him in her soft gentle voice again.

It suddenly occurred to Lord Springdale that it was how a mother should always speak to her children.

If he ever married, which he was determined not to do, and had a son, he would certainly expect his wife to talk to him in a different tone to the one she would use to anyone else.

It was something he supposed he must have heard before.

Yet it seemed to him so new and different in every way to the tone of voice of a woman who was in love or was thanking him for making her so happy.

'I would suppose,' he thought to himself, 'although it never occurred to me before, that women have a special voice for their children that is different from the way they speak to anyone who is grown up.'

It was a point that had not occurred to him before.

He thought that every word Mellina was saying to Pierre was not only attractive but something that he felt he should recognise as it was how his dear mother used to talk to him.

It was most definitely a phenomenon he had never connected with himself until now or with the women he had courted over the years.

The tone of her voice had been soft and gentle, but at the same time possessive.

It was as if she was asking him for something for which it was impossible for him to say 'no.'

The carriage then stopped beside a house where the accident had happened.

Mellina looked at Lord Springdale and said,

"I suppose we ought to go in, Ian, and explain how sorry we are that there has been an accident."

"Yes, we should do," he agreed. "Otherwise she may think that Pierre has stolen the ship that he certainly could not afford to buy."

Mellina grinned.

"It is a present he will treasure, I feel, all his life and I have never seen a child so thrilled with any gift as he is."

They pushed open the gate that led up to a rather roughly built house that was in need of paint and repair.

Lord Springdale knocked on the door.

It was opened by a woman with rolled-up sleeves and an apron, who was quite obviously either preparing a meal or cleaning the kitchen.

Speaking slowly and deliberately so that she would understand his French, because she was quite obviously a Tunisian by birth, Lord Springdale related to her what had happened.

And how they had bought Pierre a new toy ship.

She was somewhat difficult to interpret, but very grateful to them for bringing the child back and for giving him the toy as a present.

They learnt that Pierre's father was a sailor and his mother was working as a maid in this house to provide, while her husband was away, enough food for herself and the boy.

"The gentleman who lives here," she said, "is often away and, when he is, my Pierre is allowed to play in the garden. But he loves the sea and anywhere with water he goes to as if it calls to him."

"Perhaps when he grows up he will be a sailor like his father," Lord Springdale commented.

"I expect so," the woman answered, "then I'll be alone. That's what'll happen to me. Often I don't see my husband for months."

Mellina was so sorry for her.

She understood what a difficult life it must be to have a husband who was so seldom with her and who then expected her to earn sufficient money for herself and his child when he was not there to provide for them.

She glanced at Lord Springdale.

As if he knew what she was thinking, he gave the woman several pound notes which she stared at as if they were manna from Heaven.

His generosity was so amazing to her that she could hardly believe that they were for her.

"I think Pierre is a very brave little boy," Mellina said. "You must look after him and he must learn to look after you."

The woman smiled happily at her as if she had said something funny.

Then she burst into words of gratitude, which were difficult to follow.

But Mellina and Lord Springdale knew what she was saying from the expression on her face and the way she bowed to them both.

"Now we must carry on with our tour of the City," he urged Mellina.

She was kneeling on the ground helping the small boy unpack his toy ship.

Then she put her arms round him and kissed him.

"Now, Pierre, you be very careful with that ship," Lord Springdale said to him, "and don't play in the road again just in case a carriage runs over it."

"I'll take good care of it," the mother promised. "I expect he'll sleep with it in his bed and never let it out of his sight!"

"And you will have to take care of him as well," Mellina said, "and please don't allow him to play in that road again because it's so dangerous. Although we only smashed his boat, we might have run him over and really hurt him."

"I'll do my best to keep him in the garden," the woman answered. "But where there's water, that's where I'll find Pierre."

When Mellina had kissed Pierre goodbye and they drove away, Lord Springdale said to her,

"Well, you have made one little boy a very happy one and I think he will always remember the kind lady who gave him a ship."

"He was so thrilled and delighted with it," Mellina said. "I only wish that everyone we gave presents to was as grateful as he is. I think his mother is very brave."

"I think what you are saying," he replied, "is that you have no wish to marry a sailor."

"I have no wish to marry anyone," Mellina declared firmly. "But can you imagine what it would be like if you were left alone for months on end and had no idea where your husband was?"

"It is certainly a plight I would not enjoy myself, unless, of course, I was forced to marry some tiresome and idiotic woman chosen by my grandmother. Then I would be glad if she went abroad and perhaps never came back!"

"Don't think about it," Mellina said. "You know it is unlucky to think unhappy thoughts and for the moment we have both escaped and are free."

She gave a little shiver before she said,

"Last night I thought that I had got into even more trouble, but again I managed to run away. I am only scared of what might happen the third time."

"Third time lucky," Lord Springdale retorted. "As long as you can run fast enough, you will always manage to be out of reach before they catch you!"

Mellina laughed.

"It does sound funny when you think of it like that. But I was frightened last night, very very frightened."

"Tell me you will forget all about it, Mellina, and although I cannot buy you a ship to make you as happy as Pierre, at least you can be grateful to my yacht for carrying you away."

"Of course I am grateful," Mellina said. "I thank God every night in my prayers for bringing you into my life."

She smiled as she went on,

"I was only trying to joke about it rather than take seriously what has happened so far in our lives."

"We will win," he said confidently, "as we have set out to find perfect happiness in the future."

There was just a touch of sarcasm in his last words.

Then Mellina remarked,

"Because everything strange seems to happen to us, I think we are incredibly lucky. If we had stayed at home, perhaps bored, I should feel quite different from how I feel at this moment."

"How do you feel?" Lord Springdale enquired.

"Happy! Just supremely happy," Mellina answered. "Please say you are happy too, Ian."

"I am, of course, I am and in fact I can say quite honestly I am enjoying every moment of this voyage and even the weird and unexpected things that seem to happen so frequently to us."

He paused before he added,

"Perhaps one day we will put them all in a book. Then other people will be encouraged to feel as brave as we have been when we ran away."

"Of course it was brave. Nothing could have been more wonderful than the fact that you were waiting with your carriage and, when I asked you to drive off, you did so!"

Lord Springdale did not speak and Mellina carried on,

"Any other man might have been stupid enough to argue about it. Then Papa would have caught me up and I would not be here in this charming City with even more exciting events to look forward to in the future."

"There you are then," he replied, "you are making it into a story and it is something you will have to write down sooner or later. It will undoubtedly be a best-seller and all we will have to work out is a suitable title."

"You are quite right," Mellina answered.

They then drove on for a short distance when Lord Springdale said,

"We are now coming to the road of the gold and silversmiths and I am certain that they will also sell jewels. So I am going to give you a present."

"Oh, Ian, I don't want you to do that!" Mellina exclaimed.

"Pierre had a present and I must give you one too," he insisted. "Perhaps we can find something you can give me."

"I would love to," Mellina answered. "As I told you, I have brought a great deal of money with me, which I took from Papa's safe, just in case I needed it. I did not want to plead for charity to pay my fare home."

"I don't think that is likely to happen," he replied. "So do let's enjoy ourselves buying things that will always remind us of this glorious adventure together."

Mellina gave a little cry.

"Of course we must. I don't know why I did not think of it before. When we are old and grey we will say to our children, 'I must tell you how I came by this wonderful present when I was taking part in an unlikely and unusual adventure'."

Lord Springdale laughed at the obvious enthusiasm in her voice.

Then he said,

"Now you have betrayed yourself. So you *do* intend to get married."

"I suppose I must have spoken without thinking," she answered. "But it will happen to both of us eventually, because if nothing else we want to leave children behind who belong to us. Not to carry on our money or our titles, that is not of importance, but to carry on where we left off and perhaps do that much better in the world than we have managed to do."

Lord Springdale looked at her and smiled.

"You always put into words exactly what I should be thinking," he said. "You are most unusual and I have never met anyone like you before."

He hesitated for a moment before he added,

"Of course you are so right and I agree, although I think I would have argued on the other side of the case last week or any of the past years before I met you."

Mellina smiled at him.

"We are certainly advancing further and far quicker than I expected. So touch wood and let's pray that we will be as fortunate as we are at this moment."

Lord Springdale was listening intently and she went on,

"I am sure that our lives in the future will be very very wonderful because we expect them to be and we are both unbelievably lucky."

"I agree with every word you say, Mellina. Now come along, I am going to buy you the most expensive and delightful jewels that Tunis can supply and you will have to buy me something which will be as meaningful to me as Pierre's toy ship is to him."

They were both laughing as their carriage came to a standstill in the street and for a moment there only seemed to be a dazzling parade of silver and some large and rather unwieldy pieces of gold.

A little further ahead from where they had stopped Mellina saw a flash of jewels and silver and led the way into a large emporium.

They spent a great deal of time looking at objects they did not want and finding nothing which was, Mellina thought, in particularly good taste.

Then Lord Springdale found a very pretty bracelet of silver, inset with small diamonds and announced,

"This is it, Mellina. This is my present to you and it will look very lovely on your wrist."

She was delighted with the bracelet and she put it on immediately.

"Thank you, thank you," she cried. "I will keep it with me always because I think that it will bring me luck. Now I have to find something for you, Ian."

Next there was a shop that sold weapons of every description and age.

Among them was a small pistol that the shopkeeper told them proudly was the very latest weapon to come to him from Paris.

"It is what the English would call a 'revolver'," he said. "We have never had such a piece before and it can fire six times before you have to reload it."

Lord Springdale was obviously interested.

When Mellina suggested to him that it would be her present to him, he did not protest unduly.

"It is something very new and we can take it back to England to show them how up to date we are," he said. "It is a delightful gift, Mellina, and thank you very much and it could very easily come in useful, one never knows."

"The French are always so clever at designing new concepts when it comes to weapons," Mellina told him. "It is surprising that they have lost so many battles despite the fact that they have infiltrated, as they have here, into many countries and taken them over."

"They certainly have done well in this part of the world," he replied. "I suspect that they have improved the country a great deal from what it was originally."

"We have done the same in India and other places," Mellina pointed out. "But, of course, we must praise the French when they have earned it."

"From what I have heard they have done a great deal of good here," he said. "I think that they have their eyes on other parts of Africa further South."

"Well, I have to admit that I am finding Tunis very interesting," Mellina replied. "I can understand why the Romans found this a very compelling country."

"Tomorrow we will move further along the coast and see what the Romans did to Carthage," he told her. "Then, of course, we must visit the Colosseum that I have never seen myself, although I have read about it, which they built at El Djem."

"It is all very exciting," Mellina sighed, "and thank you again for my bracelet, Ian, and I am really thrilled with it."

"If you show it to David Bentley tonight," he said, "he will want to give you another one!"

Mellina smiled.

"Why should he?" she asked.

"Because he thinks that you are the most attractive young woman he has seen for a long time."

"How can you say that?" Mellina questioned him. "I only met him when we had coffee this morning."

"Perhaps he is the man you are looking for – "

They were driving back to the yacht as he spoke.

"Now you are talking nonsense," she said, "but, if he does look at me, he will see only me and not Papa's money."

"He will see a very attractive English woman," he answered. "I feel sure that he is not the least concerned with your father or what he possesses."

"Well that will be a change at any rate," Mellina replied. "Equally, as I have told you so often, I have no intention of marrying anyone until I can find my ideal man, who is very different from anyone I have come across so far."

"Then I can make plans to leave tomorrow without you weeping at the idea of leaving David Bentley behind," Lord Springdale retorted.

"You are being ridiculous!" Mellina exclaimed. "I thought he was quite pleasant, but he is certainly not my ideal. Quite frankly, I am not sure I have one."

She was looking ahead as she spoke and did not see the twinkle in Lord Springdale's eyes.

He was thinking that the women he had been with in the past would have told him that he was their ideal and all they wanted was him.

CHAPTER SIX

Mellina put on one of her prettiest gowns for dinner at the British Embassy.

Not because of what Lord Springdale had said in the morning about David Bentley but because she did not want him to be ashamed of her.

'After all,' she thought, 'as his supposed sister, he must feel that I am presentable and that he is proud of me.'

When she took a last glance at herself in the mirror, she did not see her own reflection but that of the attractive effusive woman they had encountered in Gibraltar.

Then, as it seemed fun to be going out to dinner, even though she suspected that it would be quite a small party, she took a last glance at her hair.

It looked tidy and shiny as she then picked up her chiffon handkerchief that matched her gown.

As she walked out of her cabin, Lord Springdale appeared from his at the same moment looking even smarter than he had the previous night.

He was wearing handsome jewelled buttons on his white waistcoat with a blue sash across his chest.

He looked, Mellina thought to herself, exactly as an Englishman should look when he was abroad, very smart and at the same time authoritative.

"You are very punctual," he said. "Let me tell you that that is an exceedingly pretty gown, in fact, the prettiest you have worn so far."

"I hoped that you would admire it," Mellina said, as they went up the companionway together, "because tonight we are representing Great Britain and you know only too well that foreigners always think that the British are dowdy and dull."

Lord Springdale chuckled.

"I suppose that is true of a great number of people who go abroad. But you and I are different. You are quite right that we must impress foreigners with the greatness of Great Britain and the British Empire."

"I will leave you to do that," Mellina said, as they stepped ashore and walked over to where the carriage was waiting for them.

It had been sent to the yacht from the Embassy by David Bentley.

They climbed inside and then a footman closed the doors before he jumped up beside the driver.

"This is certainly most comfortable," Mellina said as they moved off. "I am wondering who Mr. Bentley will have asked to meet us."

"I expect that he will ask someone important," Lord Springdale said, "because it is a last minute invitation and I expect that the people here, and there are a great number of French, give parties all the time and find themselves fully booked for weeks ahead."

"That is what you have when you are in London," Mellina said. "The sad part of it is that you seldom meet anyone you have not met before. Even if you do, they will all talk in much the same way and one goes home from a party thinking that it has given one nothing new or original to remember."

"The main trouble with you, Mellina, is that you are asking too much of life," he replied. "You expect the miraculous and find it very hard when you are faced with what one might call middle-class complacency."

"Now we are starting an argument!" she exclaimed. "If there is one thing I enjoy when I am with you, it is that you always say something that makes me want to argue with you and put forward a different point of view from the one you have just given."

Lord Springdale was silent for a moment obviously ruminating on what she had just said.

Then he remarked,

"I enjoy it too. In fact I find that you are the only woman I have ever come across who does not talk to me about love, which is naturally what she feels about it and it is hardly what Aphrodite offered to the world from Mount Olympus!"

Mellina gave a cry.

"Now you are saying exactly what I want to hear. But first please tell me if you have actually been to Mount Olympus, which is where I would rather go than anywhere else in the world."

"I have indeed been there," he replied, "but I found the places in Greece where the Gods still linger far more stimulating."

"Tell me about them! Do tell me," Mellina begged.

"I think, as it is a rather long story, we must keep it until another day when you are feeling bored. I will then bring up the subject of Greece as a conversation piece!"

"I think Greece means more to me than something like that," Mellina said quietly as if she was merely talking to herself. "I only hope that there are a number of books about Greece in your library on board."

"I am sure I can find you one that will answer all the questions you want to ask me," he assured her.

"But it would not be as real as listening to someone who had actually been to Mount Olympus," she replied, "and been aware that the Greek Gods still reign there."

"I think, before you say any more," he answered, "I will have to take you to Greece. But it would be rather an anticlimax if we had not first found what we are seeking elsewhere."

Mellina considered this for a moment and then she said,

"Perhaps you are right that it would be marvellous to be with someone you loved in Greece. I am sure you would feel you were being blessed by not only Aphrodite but Apollo, who I expect you know was sometimes called the 'King of Love'."

Lord Springdale smiled.

"Yes, I know. I have been to his island which I will show you if you are very good and we are still on speaking terms before our journey of discovery ends."

"Now you are being unkind to me," she protested. "You know I think you are the kindest and most wonderful man in the whole wide world to have saved me when I was really desperate and to have brought me on this exciting and thrilling adventure."

"I am not certain," he said in a somewhat sarcastic tone, "if I would call it exciting up to now, but one never knows what might happen tonight."

As he spoke, the carriage came to a halt outside the British Embassy.

The front door was opened instantly.

The light behind it seemed to stream forth so that they could find their way without any difficulty into the Embassy itself.

David Bentley was waiting for them.

As they were announced and entered the Embassy anteroom, he said with enthusiasm,

"Welcome to you both and I cannot tell you how much I was looking forward to seeing you again."

"And we are very delighted to be with you," Lord Springdale answered him.

David Bentley then took both of them into a large room where there were three other guests, already enjoying glasses of champagne.

When they were introduced to Mellina, she realised at once that they were French.

She was not in the least surprised that the woman was extremely *chic*.

Her husband was of considerable status in running the country now that it was under French control.

The third man was apparently unmarried and also French.

Although he was speaking French fluently, Mellina and Lord Springdale were told later that he was an Italian diplomat reporting to his Government in Rome about what was happening in the countries in North Africa that were now under French authority.

When they went into dinner, as David Bentley was the host in the Ambassador's absence, the French woman sat on his right and Mellina on his left.

As Lord Springdale was seated on the other side of the French woman, she immediately began to amuse him.

Not only with her repartee but with compliments she paid to England and to himself in particular.

Watching them as much as she could without being rude, Mellina thought that she was obviously the type of woman who pursued him in London.

In consequence he might find her very dull because she had no idea of how to flirt.

It was not only what the French woman said but the look in her eyes and every movement of her heavily ringed hands.

'Ian is very kind to put up with boring me,' Mellina thought.

Then she was surprised when their host said to her,

"So what are you thinking about, Miss Blakeley? You are looking sad and I cannot allow you to be sad at my party."

"I am not the least sad," Mellina replied. "In fact I am delighted to be here and to see how comfortable you are in the Embassy."

"That is because this room and the rest of the house appear to be very English," David Bentley told her, "while the kitchen, I promise you, is French and I should be very disappointed if you did not enjoy the very special dinner I have chosen for you tonight."

"I am certain it will be delicious," Mellina said. "It is very kind of you to take so much trouble over us."

"Shall I say," he answered in a low voice, "that it is trouble I have taken over *you*. I have tried to choose dishes which I think you will like and would not be able to enjoy in England."

Mellina smiled at him.

But she did not spoil his evening by telling him that they had a French chef on board the yacht, whose dishes were as good, if not better, than those she was being served at that moment.

There was no doubt, as dinner progressed, that the conversation was scintillating and intelligent.

It was certainly different from anything she would have experienced in London with girls of her own age and the young men who partnered them on the dance floor.

In fact the French made everything they said have a *double entendre*.

Lord Springdale was clearly enjoying the flirtatious words and looks of the French woman at his side.

When dinner was over, David Bentley suggested that some of them, as they were on British soil, might like to play bridge.

He then pointed out to everyone present that it was almost as much of an English pastime as cricket!

They laughed at this remark, but Mellina was aware that she was not expected to take part.

As soon as the other four guests were seated, David Bentley told her that he wished her to see the rest of the house especially the Embassy's new Picture Gallery, which they had just opened.

It contained several pictures that had been painted of Tunisia and its countryside down the centuries.

He led Mellina from the drawing room and took her upstairs to the Picture Gallery.

It was not very impressive as they had not collected many pictures as yet even though some of them were very old.

In consequence Mellina thought that they must be valuable.

She was gazing at the pictures when David Bentley came close to her and said,

"I brought you here because, as you are moving on tomorrow, I want to tell you that I must see you again."

Mellina did not answer and he went on,

"As I will be returning to England in two or three months, the one person I will want to see when I arrive in London is you."

Because he spoke to her in such an ardent manner, Mellina looked away from him and felt rather shy.

"I know it is too soon to tell you what I feel, but the moment I saw you I thought that you were different from any other woman I have ever met."

He hesitated for a moment before he continued,

"I have not been able to think of anyone else, nor will I be able to do so when you sail away as I understand from your brother that you are intending to do tomorrow morning."

Mellina had not been told that they were moving on so soon.

But she had no wish to be unkind to David, who she was sure was doing his very best to entertain them.

"What I am asking you," he said before she could speak, "is that you give me your address so that I can write to you and let you know when I am coming to London. I can only hope that you are not going to spend too long exploring the world before you head for home."

Mellina longed to tell him that the one thing she was dreading was going back to her father.

But she knew that would be a mistake.

So she merely replied,

"I will give you my address and, of course, when you come to London, my brother and I must entertain you as you have been so kind to us."

"That is what I wanted to hear," David replied. "I will try not to impose on you or unnerve you, but I knew as soon as I set eyes on you that you were the most attractive girl I have ever seen in my whole life."

"You must have met very many people," Mellina answered, "so I find that hard to believe."

"It is true," he assured her. "But I know it would be an error to try to jump my fences too quickly. So what I am asking you now is that when I come to London, which will be in about two months' time, that you will let me see you again."

Mellina drew in her breath.

But before she could speak, David went on,

"Give me your address now, Mellina, so that I can write to you and it will therefore be impossible for you to forget me before I arrive in London."

"Of course neither my brother nor I will ever forget you," Mellina said "when you have been so kind and so helpful to us on our visit to Tunis."

She thought for a moment that it would be wise to give him Lord Springdale's address rather than her own.

After all, unless everything went badly wrong and their adventure ended dismally without them finding what they were seeking, she would not be able to return home.

Her father would undoubtedly be there waiting for her with the man he considered an eligible husband.

David had produced a pen and some paper from the writing table nearby.

She wrote the address on it, which was, of course, the house in Park Lane.

"Write to me there," she said, "but I have no idea exactly when we will return to England."

"There is one thing that you must know," David said, "and that is, if you come back this way after you have visited the Colosseum of El Djem, I will be longing to see you again here in Tunis."

He spoke with an intensity that she was beginning to find somewhat embarrassing.

Swiftly Mellina replied,

"Of course we will let you know and we are very very grateful for your kindness and hospitality."

"And I am very grateful to Fate, which has brought you into my life," David answered. "There is so much I want to tell you and so much I want to talk to you about. But, if you are leaving tomorrow, I will have to wait and pray that you will not forget me when you arrive back in England."

"I promise I will not," Mellina replied.

"Then that is all I ask of you at the moment," David answered, "because I have no wish to scare you. Although I have a great deal to say, I know that I must keep it until we have known each other longer."

Feeling that she was now walking on rather delicate ground, Mellina said,

"Please let me see the rest of the Embassy as it will be something to compare with other British Embassies if we are lucky enough to be invited to them."

"I am sure wherever you go you will be invited to what is the best and the most impressive," David said, "and that is what worries me because you might well forget me."

"I will always remember how kind you have been," Mellina answered, "and as you say you will be in London in two months' time."

"I am hoping that you will be back by then," David said.

"I don't know," Mellina replied, "it all depends on Ian and I leave everything in his hands."

Because she was concerned that he might say more or perhaps try to kiss her, Mellina moved towards the door.

"Please show me the rest of the house," she asked. "We must not be too late going back to the yacht because Ian wants to start early in the morning."

"It is what everyone inevitably does when they are at sea," David replied. "I can only hope and will go on hoping, that you will call here on your way back."

Mellina thought it would be unkind to tell him that Ian was thinking of perhaps going on to Cairo.

She therefore said nothing more, merely insisting on going from room to room of the Embassy thinking that it was indeed typically English.

Most of the rooms looked very ordinary as if they had been transported straight from England into Tunisia.

Once or twice, when they were touring the rooms, she saw that David was wondering if it would be a mistake to say aloud what he was feeling.

But she managed to keep the conversation light and fairly flippant until they had finished their inspection of the Embassy.

Then David suggested that they might go into the garden.

Mellina knew at once that this would be unwise.

Without appearing eager to go back to the others, she merely said that she must find out if Ian wanted to go home.

"He lays down special rules for himself and others while he is at sea, which he does not keep when we are ashore," she said. "I must therefore do what he wants as he has been so kind in bringing me to Tunis rather than take one of his close friends with him."

David said nothing as she walked deliberately back to the room where the others were playing bridge.

They had in fact just finished a rubber.

Before they could deal out the cards yet again, Lord Springdale rose to his feet.

"Oh, here you are Mellina!" he said. "I think that we should go back to the yacht as I have told the Captain that we wish to leave at dawn. I must therefore not deprive you of your beauty sleep."

"I am sure no one could do that," the Frenchman piped up gallantly.

Mellina smiled at him.

They said goodbye and Mellina felt that she should compliment Ian on getting them away so quickly and at the same time making their host feel that they had enjoyed every single moment of the evening.

Only as they drove back towards the Port did she ask,

"Did you win your game of bridge, Ian?"

"Of course I did," Lord Springdale replied. "I am a much better player than the rest of them and I do hope that you enjoyed your tour of the Embassy. If that is what you did."

"It is indeed what we did," she said. "But David is very anxious to see us again."

"You need not include me," he retorted. "I warned you that he has fallen in love with you and the question I now have to ask is if you have fallen in love with him?"

"I think you are exaggerating what he is feeling, but he does want to see us again, Ian," Mellina said quietly. "Although I think that he is a very charming young man, I feel there is nothing very unusual or extraordinary about him, so the answer to what you are now suggesting is quite positively a 'no'!"

Lord Springdale laughed.

"Well, I am certainly relieved as I really don't want to have to go on to Carthage alone. I was half-afraid, as I was beating them all at bridge, that I should find myself travelling to the Colosseum of El Djem to be punished as the Romans used to punish their prisoners without your protection."

"They punished their prisoners," Mellina answered, "by feeding them to the lions and tigers and I believe that even you would find that somewhat difficult to combat!"

"Unless, of course, you are there to protect me," he replied jokingly, "as you protected me in London and I hope that you have not forgotten that you have promised to protect me again if it proves necessary."

"I only hope I will be able to do so," Mellina said. "Although David Bentley has been very kind to us, I am glad we are leaving him behind."

Lord Springdale looked at her questioningly.

She was aware he was doing so by the moonlight streaming in through the windows of the carriage.

"No! No! No!" Mellina emphasised. "I know exactly what you are asking me and the answer is 'no'!"

He laughed.

"Well, at least you have to admit that he was not thinking of your father's money. Quite frankly I think that you might do worse than marry him, which would prevent you from being troubled as you might be when you return home."

"We have not yet come to the end of our voyage," she said, "and until we do I refuse to be rushed into doing anything that would be a mistake and the worst one either of us could make would be to marry someone we did not love and who did not love us with the real love we have set out to find."

She spoke as if the words came from her very heart.

Lord Springdale then said,

"Forgive me, I was only teasing you. Of course we have not yet found what we set out to find. But because I am an optimist I believe that we will be lucky even when we least expect it."

"I do hope you are right," Mellina replied in a small voice. "But perhaps we are asking too much of the Gods – who watch over us."

"Who have brought us this far in safety," he added. "So we must not belittle them, but trust them to bring us what we pray for even though they may take a little time in doing so."

Mellina smiled.

As the carriage turned to drive down the road that led to the Port, she slipped her hand into his.

"We will win, I just know we will win!" Mellina exclaimed. "We must not lose heart when we have come so far."

Lord Springdale's fingers tightened over hers.

"You are quite right," he sighed. "We will go on hoping that tomorrow will be the marvellous day when we finally discover what we are seeking – "

He stopped for a moment before he went on,

"Because we both believe in Fate I feel sure that we will find it."

"Of course – we will," Mellina whispered.

He knew from the way she spoke that she was far more certain of it than she had been previously.

*

They moved out of Tunis and arrived in Carthage at midday.

They had brushed up their knowledge of the ancient City over breakfast.

Lord Springdale told her how it had been at one time a great Metropolis from where the Romans had governed the whole of North Africa.

While he was telling her all that he knew, he found that Mellina, having read more research books than he had, was aware that the Romans had built a Colosseum here at Carthage to rival the one at El Djem.

It was here that they brought their enemies into the arena naked to be slaughtered and they had also at one time sacrificed a great number of children.

"It was so cruel," Mellina said, "that I have no wish to see the Colosseum here, although I expect the other one will be almost as bad."

"Amongst these ruins there is very little left of the Colosseum or of the fine houses that must have been most impressive in their time," he remarked. "Quite frankly, as I think there is very little we want to see and what you have just told me will obviously upset you, we will move on."

He therefore told the Captain that they were no longer interested in seeing Carthage and would travel on to El Djem where there were horses waiting to carry them to the great Colosseum they both wanted to see.

As he gave the orders, he thought that they would certainly enjoy being able to ride after being cooped up in the yacht for so long.

He had never discussed horses with Mellina.

But he had a feeling that she would be an excellent horsewoman, although he was rather uncertain as to why he was so sure of it.

Having left Carthage behind, they travelled swiftly in smooth water towards Mahdia, a fishing village nearest to the Colosseum at El Djem.

They arrived when it was dusk and there was no question of going ashore.

At the same time the harbour of the small fishing village seemed somehow to welcome them with its multi-coloured twinkling lights.

"This place seems quite different from Tunis," he said. "I don't know why, but there is an atmosphere about it which makes you believe in Fairy stories."

They were standing on the deck of the yacht as he spoke and Mellina turned to look at him in surprise.

Then she said,

"And I was thinking the same. It is quite a different atmosphere even though the Romans were undoubtedly as cruel here as they were at Carthage."

"Forget that," he urged. "Think how marvellous it is that this amazing Colosseum has survived all through the centuries when it was so badly neglected. It is only now that the tourists are visiting it and, of course, people like ourselves who are always looking for something different to explore."

Mellina laughed.

"I suppose that is true and maybe we ask too much. But I have a distinct feeling that this Colosseum will tell us the secret that it has kept for so long of bringing the world hope when everyone is feeling low and near to despair."

Lord Springdale thought that she was talking of her own deeply held feelings.

He put his hand on her shoulder.

"Always remember that tomorrow will be brighter than today and will bring you what you most desire," he said.

"That is what I am trying to decipher," she replied. "I agree with you that there seems something in the air or maybe it is just magic that is different here from anywhere else we have been."

"Tomorrow I would suggest that we have an early breakfast and leave as soon as we have finished it," he said.

He gazed again at the harbour lights before he went on,

"It is a long ride, but they have told me that the Colosseum of El Djem is still wonderful and perhaps it will give us new hope and a renewed conviction that however difficult the path may be we will eventually find what we are seeking."

"I am sure we will," she murmured. "But nothing could be more beautiful than where we are now."

As she spoke, she looked up at the sky where the stars were shining down on the little fishing village.

As the anchor went down, Mellina threw back her head and looked up towards the moon.

"What do you see?" Lord Springdale asked her.

"I am praying that we will find here what we both wish for and that of course – is real happiness," she said very quietly.

He thought as he listened that only Mellina could say that with such sincerity that he was forced to agree with her.

Once again he was thinking that she was so very different from any other woman he had ever known.

CHAPTER SEVEN

Mellina was woken very early by Lord Springdale knocking on her door.

She realised that he was up and about already and she must not keep him waiting.

So she hurriedly jumped out of bed and washed and dressed herself in what she felt must be record time.

She went up to the Saloon where Lord Springdale was already eating his breakfast.

"You are very early," she commented. "I was fast asleep when you knocked."

"I was afraid that you might be," he told her. "But unless we get off as soon as possible, we shall run into the crowds which come up from the South. I want to see the Colosseum of El Djem, as indeed you do, without mobs of people making a noise as they wander over it."

"Of course you are right, Ian. It would be a mistake to see anything that we have been told is so beautiful with crowds of sightseers filling it."

"I doubt if they would do that," he answered, "but they would certainly be a nuisance."

He smiled at her as he continued,

"As you know, I have arranged for our horses to be waiting for us here."

Mellina had dressed in her riding skirt, but she had thought it quite unnecessary, as it was very hot, for her to wear anything but the blouse that went with it.

She finished eating breakfast as quickly as possible and then she ran down to her cabin to collect her hat.

She carried it in her hand and, as Lord Springdale looked at it rather questioningly, she said,

"I shall only wear it when the sun gets really hot. I love feeling the cool morning breeze on my face. And a hat, however small it is, always seems to make one feel overdressed."

He laughed.

"I never thought of that. Perhaps I don't need a hat either."

He threw down the Panama hat he was holding in his hand.

They walked along the gangway and onto the rough quay of the fishing village of Mahdia.

They had to climb a little up from the sea to where the horses were stabled on the outskirts of the village.

Mellina was thrilled to find that the horses were far better than she had expected.

The two which had been kept for them, because the order had come directly from the British Embassy, were both extremely solid horses that she was quite certain could be persuaded to go pretty fast.

"You be very early, sir," the groom said, speaking somewhat bad French. "But the crowds be comin' from the South later on and you be wise to see the Colosseum before it is filled with them."

"That is what I thought myself," Lord Springdale replied. "And thank you for providing us with such good horses."

"They be the best and no mistake about it," the man answered. "But you be careful you don't meet one of them mad Bedouins as has been hangin' about recently."

Lord Springdale was not paying attention to what he was saying, but Mellina asked him,

"Why are they mad and what do they do?"

"They frighten them horses for one thing," the man replied. "In fact, they made one horse rear so high that he threw off the man who be ridin' him. Then the horse came runnin' back here with no one in the saddle."

"I hope it does not happen to us," Mellina gasped.

"Well then, you look out for them. There be two I understands carryin' on round here and naturally what they wants be money!"

Mellina smiled.

"That is just what far too many people want in the world," she said.

The man did not answer as he was helping her into the saddle.

As she then picked up the reins, she thought how exciting it was to be riding with Lord Springdale.

It was what she hoped to do when they went back to England.

Yet even to think of home made her shudder.

She felt quite certain that her father would still be waiting to force her into marrying that dreadful man he had chosen for her.

She recognised that he would be even more abusive about it because she had stolen away from him without his permission.

Lord Springdale was already mounted on his horse and, as he rode out of the stable, he called out,

"Come along! The sooner we get there the better we shall see it. As it is, we have a long way to go."

As he was speaking, he touched his horse gently and it sprang forward and Mellina had to make every effort to catch up with him.

Then they were riding side by side and she thought that nothing could be more enthralling.

She had no idea how entrancing she looked with the sun gleaming on her fair hair and her thin blouse rippling a little in the wind.

Looking at her now, Lord Springdale thought that he might have guessed that she would indeed be a superb rider.

She was actually far better on horseback than any woman he had ever seen.

He then spurred his own horse to keep ahead of her.

Eventually they rode up to the Colosseum at what he was quite certain was at a pace none of the usual tourists would achieve.

Because they had started so early and because they rode so quickly, despite the fact that they were continually going uphill, they arrived at the entrance to the Colosseum before any of the other visitors.

In fact the man who was waiting to take the horses from them, said,

"You be early, sir, we ought to give you a prize for being the first here today."

"I should be pleased to receive it," Lord Springdale replied, "and we shall very likely leave before you become too crowded. Please give the horses a drink. They deserve it, as they came up the hill in what I am quite certain was a record speed."

"Oh! So you've got the good ones today," the man remarked. "Some of the horses they send are so rocky on their legs they couldn't climb a molehill, let alone this here mountain!"

"We are pleased to have done it. Now we will go and view the Colosseum of El Djem in all its glory."

He patted his horse as he spoke.

Then he joined Mellina, who was already gazing at the Colosseum and waiting somewhat impatiently for him.

They moved quickly, thinking how essential it was to see as much as they could before it was spoilt by visitors who would doubtless have noisy children running about.

Mellina looked round and realised that, as she had read in one of Lord Springdale's books, the Colosseum had been built in the second century A.D. and when finished could hold an astonishing thirty thousand people.

Now the terraces and pillars were overgrown with grass and flowers.

Yet she thought that it still had the style and glory it originally must have had when it became the second largest Colosseum that the Romans ever built after Rome.

They walked down a little way and then sat on a terrace so that they would see the way that the people could view the proceedings when the Colosseum was completed.

Now the flowers, the grass and the bright sunshine made it beautiful rather than intimidating.

It was impossible to think about the agony of those who had suffered and died here.

Mellina also remembered, because she had read it very carefully in Lord Springdale's books when she knew where they were going, how in 1695 Mohammed Bey had destroyed the North side of the Colosseum in order to drive out the supporters of a rival tribe.

The book said that it made it possible to study how the vast amphitheatre had been designed and constructed by the Romans.

It was one hundred and twelve feet high and nearly three hundred and ten feet long. Prisoners of war, slaves, bankrupts, criminals and Christians, who were fed to the lions, were all persecuted and killed here.

But, as it was so beautiful, Mellina did not want, at this moment, to think about the appalling horrors that had taken place on this site.

Or the misery caused by the deaths through the ages of thousands and thousands of people.

Instead, as the sun was shining so brightly, the bees were humming over the flowers and the butterflies moved in front of them.

They then climbed down towards the lower level.

She thought that the Colosseum was almost a Fairy story in itself.

Because she was now gazing round her from side to side, Lord Springdale said to her,

"I knew this would thrill you, Mellina. It is at the moment stunningly beautiful instead of being horrible and blood-stained."

"I don't think about the past," she said, "it is just so exciting to see a building that has lasted so long and which has made people interested in the Romans even though we cannot think that their ways were decent or commendable."

They reached the lowest level and, as they did so, Mellina said,

"I must see where the lions were kept. I wonder how many there were?"

She did not wait for Lord Springdale to answer.

She ran over to the side of the Colosseum where she could see that there were large holes in the walls like the entrance to caves.

She peeped into the first one.

It was very dark and she could see nothing, so she went into the second one.

Lord Springdale had moved to take a closer look at the side that had been demolished and thought it a pity that the Colosseum had not been allowed to remain as it had been when it had first been built.

He was staring at some rocks that were heaped on the ground when he heard Mellina scream and then turned round.

There was no sign of her, but she screamed again, and he ran towards the opening where her cry had come from.

As he entered the cave, he saw that she was being held round the waist by a very strange looking man.

He was half-naked and was clearly a Bedouin.

He was obviously the mad man who had frightened the horse that had thrown its rider and galloped back to its stable.

Lord Springfield saw that Mellina could not escape from the Bedouin and he was holding a large knife in his hand and was pointing it at her throat.

"Give me money!" he called out in a rough voice in French, so that it was difficult to understand what he was saying. "Money! Money! Or I kill her!"

Lord Springdale's left hand went immediately into the inner pocket of the riding coat he was wearing.

At the same moment, his right hand went into his outside pocket, where he had put before he left the yacht, the new revolver, the present that Mellina had given him in Tunis.

And he had been wise enough to load it with six bullets before they had set out to visit the Colosseum of El Djem.

He pulled with his left hand at some large notes and, as the mad man stared at them, he shot with his right hand at his shoulder above the arm he was holding Mellina captive with.

His scream seemed to echo in the cave, as he fell backwards when the bullet hit him.

Mellina, now free of the mad man's arms, managed to run to Lord Springdale and flung herself against him.

He had already slipped the revolver back into his coat pocket and he held her close to him.

"It's quite all right, my darling," he said soothingly. "You are safe. He will not hurt you now."

Then he was not quite certain how it happened, but somehow, as he was speaking, his lips found Mellina's.

As he kissed her, he knew that this was different in every way from how he had ever kissed.

As he could feel her body trembling against him, he thought that she as well had felt the strange and unexpected ecstasy as their lips touched.

Just for a moment they were quite still.

Then, whilst the man on the ground groaned, Lord Springdale took Mellina's hand and pulled her outside the cave.

Without speaking, they started to climb the terraces back up to the top.

He went so quickly that once or twice she stumbled and was only saved when he put his arm round her.

They then reached the entrance to the Colosseum and just outside it was the shelter where their horses were kept.

There was no sign of the man they had left them with, but there was water in front of both horses so he had obeyed Lord Springdale's instructions.

He put two gold coins down beside one of the water buckets.

And then he lifted Mellina onto her saddle.

As she rode out of the shelter, he mounted his own horse and followed her.

They did not speak.

But Lord Springdale gradually increased the pace until they were moving downhill much faster than they had climbed up.

At the same time, because it was still so early in the morning, there was no one to notice them.

They rode on without saying a word before finally the little fishing village of Mahdia came into sight.

They then went into the stable from where they had hired their horses.

The groom looked at them in surprise.

"You're back early, sir," he said. "Weren't it what you expected?"

"We saw the Colosseum and then found it better to come home before the crowds appeared," Lord Springdale answered him.

As he spoke, Mellina slipped down from her horse and then walked along the path to the harbour where the yacht was anchored.

After she went aboard, she headed straight for her cabin without waiting for Lord Springdale to follow her.

She was still suffering from shock at being seized by the mad Bedouin.

And the horror she felt when she heard him say that he would kill her if they did not give him money.

'Just how could I have been so stupid?' she asked herself, 'as to go straight into the lion's den.'

But all that she had been able to think about as she was riding back had been the kiss that Ian had given her and the mysterious and wonderful feelings it had aroused in her.

No man had ever kissed Mellina before, but she had known that that was how a kiss should be.

It was even different to what she had imagined it would be.

Because it was still so early, in fact, too early for breakfast, she thought that she would be wise to lie down and would not have to face the world until it was far later in the day.

Quickly she took off her riding clothes and, putting on one of the pretty nightgowns that her mother had always worn, she slipped into bed.

She felt somehow that, because Ian had kissed her, she did not want to see him for the moment or to discuss what had happened.

It was all in a muddle in her mind and all she could think of was the glorious wonder she had felt when his lips had touched hers.

She was lying on her pillows thinking of his kiss and feeling that at last she understood why people talked so much about love – if love was as heavenly as this.

There as a knock at the door and Ian came into her cabin.

"I thought you would be sensible enough," he said, "to lie down after that unpleasant experience. However, I will always, as I think that you will, Mellina, remember the Colosseum of El Djem!"

Mellina did not answer.

She sat up and could only gaze wide-eyed at him as he came towards her.

She had no idea now beautiful she looked with the sun from the portholes glinting on her hair and turning it to burnished gold.

Her eyes were wide and to Ian they were expressing what he was feeling.

To her surprise he sat down on the bed and said,

"There are no words to say and so I will not express to you yet what I am feeling."

He bent forward as he spoke and, as he kissed her, she felt again that strange marvellous inexpressible feeling of wonder that had swept through her when he had kissed her in the Colosseum.

Only now, as his lips became more demanding and even more passionate, she knew that this was what she had been seeking and what she had always believed love would be like.

'*I love you*! I love you!' she wanted to shout to Ian.

But he kissed her until it was impossible for her to say anything.

When at last he raised his head, she then heard the yacht's anchor being drawn up.

The wheels of the engine were turning beneath her.

"Are we going – away?" she managed to ask him in a whisper.

It was difficult to say anything as Ian was so close to her.

"We are going as quickly as possible to Athens," he answered.

She stared at him.

"We are going to be married, my darling," he told her.

"*Married*!"

Mellina was not even certain if she said the words or only thought them.

"I love you," Ian said. "I love you as I thought love would be and I was afraid I would never find it. I believe you love me too!"

"I love you! I love you!" Mellina murmured. "But I did not know that love could ever be – so wonderful or so sublime."

"That is what we must always make it," Ian said. "And my darling one, are you quite sure you want to marry me?"

"I thought you would never – ask me that question. You were so certain, and so was I, that we would find love, but – in a different way."

"We have found love in the only right way," he told her. "We know what we both mean to each other. I think I realised that you were the one woman I wanted as my wife when I saw you cuddling little Pierre and soothing him when he was so frightened."

Mellina smiled.

"I was thinking that if I ever had a child – I would protect him and make quite certain – that he was not run over or endangered in any way," she said.

"When did you first know that you loved me?" Ian asked.

Mellina looked shy.

"I did not know that it was love then, but I was very frightened at Gibraltar when that beautiful lady talked to you and I thought that maybe you would send me home alone."

"I am not so crazy as to do anything like that," Ian said. "But I think I fell in love with you when you did not succumb to the rough waves in the Bay of Biscay."

She laughed.

"I cannot think that was something to make you fall in love."

"No, no, of course not, but you were so different in every way from every other woman I have ever known."

He smiled lovingly at her.

"In fact," he continued, "I must have been crazy not to realise sooner that you are *my* woman. You belong to me and I swear that I will never let you go."

Then, before Mellina could answer, he was kissing her again, kissing her until she felt as if they were flying up into the sky into everlasting sunshine.

*

Later that day when they were speeding through the Mediterranean, Ian took her up on deck and they went to their favourite place where they could talk and gaze at the beauty of the sea at the same time.

There was a sofa there as well as chairs.

Ian drew her close to him with his arm around her.

"Now we must make plans," he said. "I know that you want to go to Mount Olympus and I want to show you the other places in Greece that are connected with love, including, of course, the island where Apollo was born."

"You know what that would mean to me," Mellina said in a soft voice. "You are quite certain that you want to marry me, Ian – having said that you would never marry – anyone?"

"I am quite, quite certain that I want to marry you," Ian replied, "and I could well ask the same question of you, my darling one, although you can hardly expect me to be interested in your father's money."

"And I am not marrying you for your title," Mellina said, "because to me, you have always been the kindest, the most wonderful man imaginable and – I still cannot believe that I am lucky enough to have found you."

She gave a deep sigh before she added,

"How could I know that, when I was running away from the horrible man Papa wanted me to marry, I would jump into what I believed was a hired carriage and find *you*?"

"I think that the Gods who look after us in Heaven planned that we should meet and, as we were brave enough to run away together, we did as they told us and this is the result."

"I am so afraid that one day you may regret having married me, Ian, when we really do know – so little about each other."

It was impossible to say anything more because Ian had tipped her face up to his and was kissing her.

Kissing her once again until the wonder and rapture of it was so intense that, when he took his lips from hers, she merely hid her face against his shoulder.

"That is the answer to all your questions," he said. "If you can feel like that and make me feel the same way, we have won our victory and there is nowhere further for us to go."

"I – love you. I love you," Mellina whispered.

Then there was no need for either of them to say any more.

*

They were married that evening after the yacht had moved into the Port of Athens.

Ian recalled that there was a small Anglican Chapel near to the British Embassy, which he had noticed on one occasion years ago when he was visiting Greece.

He had in fact inspected it, because it was very old, and he had met the Clergyman who was in charge of it.

He found to his surprise that he was English.

"I came here many years ago when I was a boy," he told him, "and I was determined to come back. They had a lot of difficulty finding a Priest, who would bury himself in Greece, but I was eager to accept the position and I have now been here now for over twenty-seven years."

Because he had been particularly interested in the Chapel itself, which had stood there for centuries, Ian had given him quite a substantial sum to preserve it when he had left.

And his generosity was not forgotten.

When he then went ashore in Athens to arrange his marriage, he was so delighted to find that the elderly Priest was still there and only too pleased to marry them that very evening.

When he returned to the yacht, Mellina was waiting for him.

She ran down the deck as soon as he came aboard.

"We are being married this evening," Ian told her with a broad smile on his face.

"This evening!" she exclaimed in astonishment.

"I just cannot wait any longer to make you mine," he went on, "so go and put on your best dress. There are several arrangements that I wish to make."

She could not argue with him, even though she had no wish to do so.

As he disappeared in the direction of the bridge, she knew that she must do as he wanted.

She went to her cabin where she had already found amongst her clothes a white dress that was very becoming and had once belonged to her mother.

It had been made in Paris and so was beautifully designed in white chiffon with very fine lace.

When she had put it on, she knew that she looked just as smart as if she was going to a ball at Buckingham Palace.

'I really want Ian to remember his wedding,' she told herself, 'because he is so marvellous, his wife must be really beautiful and worthy of him.'

After he left her, she had prayed from the bottom of her heart that she would be a good wife and would, of course, give him the sons he wanted.

'I love him! I adore him!' she carried on saying to herself. 'How can I be so lucky to have found anybody so glorious.'

Ian had told her how he had arranged for their Wedding to take place in an hour's time.

"I can be ready," Mellina said, "if you are quite certain that you are not doing anything – in a hurry, which you might regret later?"

"I know that I shall never regret marrying you, my darling," Ian said. "I have been looking for you all my life and now that I have found you I am not going to waste any more time. But I will seize my happiness while I have the chance."

"It is so wonderful, so marvellous for me," Mellina sighed. "But I should hate you to think that I pushed you into doing something that you might regret later."

Ian merely laughed.

"If you think you and I are going to regret marrying one another, you are completely wrong. We have found what we set out to find and to query it in any way would, I think, be insulting to those who have led us to the ecstatic happiness we are feeling now."

He drew her closer to him as he finished speaking and whispered in her ear,

"You are quite certain that I am the wonderful man you were looking for? I was so concerned that he might have been David from the Embassy."

"You are merely fishing for compliments," Mellina answered. "I love you! I love you! You fill all my dreams as you always will."

Ian kissed her and then there was no reason to say anything more.

Wearing her white dress with a soft veil over her hair held by a wreath of small white roses, Mellina and Ian slipped away from the yacht.

In fact they felt that no one on board had realised that they had gone.

Actually the Captain had been let into their secret by Ian, but Mellina was not aware of this until later.

There was a large carriage waiting to carry them to the Chapel and they sat side by side, holding hands.

There was a pretty bouquet of white orchids on the seat opposite them that seemed to Mellina to symbolise their happiness.

They were feeling that there was nothing they could say because they were both so exquisitely happy.

They were reaching towards the sky with the angels watching and protecting them.

When they entered the small Chapel, Mellina was surprised to see that it was filled with white flowers that scented the air.

She learnt later that they had been ordered by Ian.

The old Priest then read the Marriage Service very simply, but it was with a sincerity that was very moving.

When they knelt to be blessed by him, Mellina was sure that the angels were singing and that God was blessing them too.

When the Service was over, they drove back to the yacht.

Holding hands, there was still no need for words.

They were both living in a heavenly circle.

Their love seemed to vibrate through their bodies as if Heaven was opening for them.

When they stepped aboard, they were piped by two sailors and the Captain came forward to wish them every happiness.

Dinner was waiting for them in the Saloon, which was massed with white flowers.

Mellina learnt that the crew were celebrating their wedding on Ian's explicit orders and were drinking their health below decks.

The chef had spent the day cooking them a wedding cake that was in Mellina's mind as beautiful as the flowers that scented the Saloon.

They were almost too happy to eat the delicious food that he had cooked for them.

But they did their best rather than hurt his feelings in refusing anything.

Then, when dinner was over, they walked together on deck to look at the lights of Athens and the moon and stars overhead.

"It has been a very quick Wedding," Mellina said, "but still a very moving and spiritual one."

"Do you really mean that?" Ian asked her.

"Would I tell you anything that was not true at this – magic moment," she murmured.

"I want you to always remember this day," he said. "I know I shall always remember the Service in that little Chapel and the Priest I shall always think of as one of the most dedicated men I have ever met."

"The Service was so inspiring," Mellina agreed. "I shall – think of it often."

"That is just what I want you to do," he answered. "And now, my darling, as we are both tired after this long day, I think we should retire to bed."

She knew what he was saying and blushed a little before she turned away.

Then, when she would have entered her own cabin, Ian opened the Master bedroom and she saw that not only was it decorated with flowers that scented the air but also that all her clothes had been moved while they were having dinner from her single cabin into the large one.

For a moment she could only look around her and think how beautiful the cabin was with all the flowers and the light of the moon streaming in through the porthole.

Ian had disappeared and she guessed that he had gone into the cabin that she had used previously.

One of her prettiest nightgowns was lying on the bed.

She quickly took off her wedding dress and hung it up in the cupboard.

Then, when she had pulled on her nightgown and was in bed, the door opened and Ian came in.

He did not say anything, but walked to the bed and stood looking down at her so that she felt shy.

Then he said very softly,

"This is the most perfect and sublime night of my life. I love you and you love me and we both suffered and struggled to find each other. Now this is our reward and could anything be more divine?"

Because she could not think of what to say in reply, except that she loved him, she held out her arms.

As he climbed into the bed beside her, she knew that this was what they had both longed for and believed that they would never find.

"I love you! I adore you!" Ian said over and over again.

Then, as very gently he made her his, she knew that they had both reached the Heaven that is always waiting for lovers if only they have the strength and persistence to find it.

As the night darkened, there was no sound but the soft lap of the sea against the side of the yacht.

Mellina fell asleep in Ian's arms thinking that they had both found the perfection of Heaven.

CHAPTER EIGHT

The next morning when Mellina awoke, she found that Ian was looking down at her as she lay in bed.

The sun was streaming in through the portholes and she realised they had slept peacefully through the night.

"Do you still love me?" he asked her.

Mellina smiled.

"I think that I must have been dreaming about you, which was stupid of me, when you have been beside me – all the time."

"I have been asleep too," he said, "only because I was so happy I could hardly believe that I was still here on this earth."

He kissed her very gently and then told her,

"Now you and I are going to find out more about love than we know already."

Mellina's eyes widened.

"What do you mean by that?" she asked.

"I mean," he said, "that our honeymoon is going to be very different from the one I might have promised you when you came aboard."

"I think you said that you were taking me to see the Pyramids to start with," Mellina replied.

"They can wait until another time. Because we are in Greece I want to go on exploring this wonderful love we have found together and where else can we learn about it except in Greece?"

Mellina gave a little cry of delight.

"If you really mean that, I think it would be more thrilling than anything else we could ever do. As you say, the rest of the world can wait."

As they were talking, she realised that the engines were turning and they were now moving out of the Port of Athens.

"Where are we going first?" she asked her husband.

"There is so much of Greece I want to show you that I can only think that it will be very difficult to find all the Temples of Love where the Greeks worshipped."

When they had finished making their plans, and Ian had once more taken Mellina in his arms to show her his love for her, they climbed slowly out of bed.

They dressed and had their breakfast as the sun was beginning to increase the warmth of the day.

Because Ian was looking for the origin of love, he took Mellina first to Delphi.

He told her how Apollo, the God of Love, had left the Holy Island of Delos to conquer Greece and a dolphin had guided his ship to the town of Crisa which was situated beneath its Shining Cliffs.

"The young God leapt from the ship disguised as a star at high noon," he told her. "The flames soared from him and a flash of splendour filled the sky. The star then vanished and there was only a youngster armed with a bow and a quiver of arrows."

"How wonderful," Mellina said a little breathlessly just thinking that she was looking at Apollo himself in the shape of Ian.

"Apollo marched up the steep road to the lair of the dragon that guarded the cliffs," Ian continued, "and, when the dragon was slain, he announced in a clear ringing voice to the Gods that he was now claiming possession of all the territory he could see from where he was standing."

Mellina was thrilled to stand on what Ian told her was the actual place where the God had stood and then to walk up towards the Shining Cliffs.

*

On another day, as they moved between the islands, Ian decided to take her to Olympia.

The low curving hills around Olympia suggested a great calm. The two nearby Cities of Elis and Pisa claimed possession of the site and then waged war for the right to control the Games.

But, as they were looking round, Ian told Mellina,

"In the year 779 BC peace was established and in that summer the first Games were opened. Eventually all the great Princes of Greece attended the Games and the tyrants of Italy and Sicily came in gilded barges."

Mellina was in raptures to think how all that she had read in the history books was coming to life in front of her.

"Aeschylus, Sophocles, Euripides and even Pindar recited their poetry here," Ian related, "and Herodotus read his histories aloud. Even the Gods took part in the Games, and the victorious included the great Apollo, who managed to brilliantly outdistance Hermes at running."

"We are never far from Apollo, the God of Love, are we?" Mellina pointed out. "He means so much to both of us."

As she stood listening to Ian, her hand was in his and they were as close to each other as they could possibly be.

Then Ian said gently,

"Do you feel, my darling, the holiness and wonder that the Gods gave to the world is still in the air?"

"I feel that it is wonderful and marvellous because I am close to you," Mellina said. "But I feel also that the love, which started here, has gradually spread throughout the world and that is why other people like us are drawn to Greece."

*

The day after leaving Olympia, Ian took Mellina to the one place that she had always wanted to visit, the island of Delos.

In ancient times it was a virgin island where no one was allowed to be born or to die or fall sick.

Mellina was immediately aware of the strange light that fell over the island.

At first she felt the effect of strangeness, even of unreality.

Then Ian could see in her face that she was now basking in the light from the other islands flooding Delos in brightness.

Delos lay very low on the water with only the small hill of Cynthus to hold it from floating away.

Mellina drew in her breath at the sheer beauty of the island, at the blue and violet sea that washed its shores and the winds blowing fresh and sweet that just ruffled her golden hair.

Ian was thinking that she made an ethereal picture and that the Gods would be admiring her sublime beauty.

There were masses of flowers with whole sheets of anemones flooding all the meadows that were filled with ancient columns and endless piles of ruins gleaming in the hot Mediterranean sun.

Mellina bent down to touch the cascades of flowers with the tips of her fingers, as if they were magical.

Ian felt that he had never in his life seen anything so beautiful as the kaleidoscope of flowers and the spiritual light that seemed to emanate from them.

"The islands round about here," Ian told her, "are called by the Greeks, the Cyclades, 'the wheeling ones', as they seem to wheel around this small island of Apollo as it stood lonely in their midst."

"It's all really fascinating," Mellina cried. "Do you know any more about it?"

"Yes," Ian answered. "It is said that to celebrate the birth of Apollo, the islands wheeled round in Holy joy, strange and exotic perfumes filled the air and white swans suddenly appeared on the lake."

"I can just imagine the scene," Mellina whispered.

"Leto, the mother of Apollo, gave him ambrosia and nectar and he grew up tall and straight."

"Just like you," Mellina told Ian as she looked at him with all her love for him in her eyes.

Mellina could now see above him the strange light, glittering and shining high up in the air.

It was almost as if she could hear the beating of Apollo's silver wings and feel the whirling of his silver wheels.

"This is the spot where Apollo was born," she said in awe. "I never believed that I would ever come here – with my own Apollo."

With reluctance they felt they would have to leave the island which had touched both their hearts.

As they turned to leave, Mellina sighed to Ian,

"I could never have believed that anything could be more incredibly beautiful or more inspiring than – all that you have shown me today."

They returned to the yacht thrilled and awed by all that they had seen and felt.

When they made love that night, they both felt as if they were being carried away on silver wings to the stars and were surrounded by myriads of flowers.

The next morning Ian leant over to Mellina in the bed to whisper in her ear,

"There is just one more place I want to take you, my darling. And that is the island of Rhodes."

When they landed there, Mellina remembered that Rhodes was known as Apollo's playground.

"What happened here," she began to tell Ian, "is that, whilst Apollo was driving his sun-chariot across the Heavens, the Gods drew lots to divide up the earth among themselves."

She smiled at him, but he did not say anything.

"Apollo was furious and stormed in to tell the Gods that the earth would have to be divided up again," she went on. "Suddenly he espied a beautiful island lurking at the far end of the shining sea."

"What did he do then?" Ian enquired.

"He was so excited at the beauty of this island," Mellina replied, "that he offered to let all the other Gods keep their possessions as long as this one island was given to him."

"And this happened?"

"It did and then Apollo bathed the island in his own radiance, enriched it with many precious gifts and named it after his sacred flower, the rose."

"That is marvellous," Ian enthused. "You certainly know all about it, my darling Mellina."

They took their time wandering around the island, finally coming to the ancient town of Lindos near to where the yacht was anchored.

They had left the high blue mountains behind them gleaming in the sunshine and the broad valley of Rhodes carpeted with flowers.

The wild jagged coastline then swung inwards and suddenly before them they saw, rising abruptly between the shining waters of two bays, high on a hill, the pillars of the ancient Temple of Athene, standing like sentinels at the very edge of the cliffs.

"Nothing in the world exists like this," Ian told her, "the dark blue of the sea and this Temple, which had once stood high up in the sky, shining out like a beacon."

They were standing close together, holding hands, and Mellina was now staring at what were now the only remaining columns of the Temple.

Before her very eyes it became transformed as if by Apollo himself.

She could now see the whole of the magnificent Temple, gleaming purest white in the sunshine, surrounded by small puffs of cloud.

This was a vision and yet Mellina could see it all quite clearly.

There was Athene, the greatest Goddess of all time, standing in the centre of her own Temple, throwing out her hands towards Mellina and then the three other Gods were doing the same.

It was a moment of such exquisite beauty and she felt as if she herself was no longer on earth.

And there right before her very eyes the Gods were blessing Ian and her and their everlasting love for each other.

Then she was aware that Ian was putting his arms round her and kissing her in the strange marvellous way as when he had kissed her for the first time.

She knew that it meant that he had seen what she had just seen.

Then, as Ian held her closer still, she felt as if they were one being and not two.

She knew that the child held within her would be a boy and that he would take a perfect place in the world and would bring happiness to a great many people.

It was a moment that she would always remember in her soul because it proved unmistakably that what they were feeling was the love that came from God, was a part of God and would be theirs for all Eternity.